THE
PORTRAIT

Liz Woodhouse

THE
PORTRAIT

LIZ WOODHOUSE

Matador
Unit E2 Airfield Business Park,
Harrison Road, Market Harborough,
Leicestershire. LE16 7UL
Tel: 0116 2792299
Email: books@troubador.co.uk
Web: www.troubador.co.uk/matador
Twitter: @matadorbooks

ISBN 978 1803131 351

British Library Cataloguing in Publication Data.
A catalogue record for this book is available from the British Library.

Printed and bound in Great Britain by 4edge Limited
Typeset in 11pt Minion Pro by Troubador Publishing Ltd, Leicester, UK

Matador is an imprint of Troubador Publishing Ltd

To Alice, Matt, and Catherine

Tudor family tree

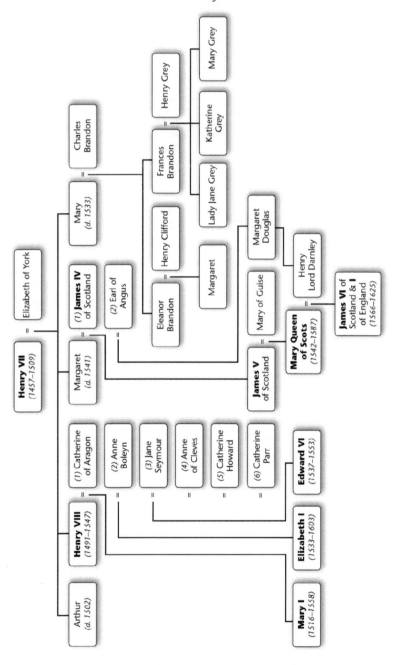

GREENWICH PALACE, CHRISTMAS 1545

Two guardsmen stand at the door to Lady Elizabeth's quarters. They watch as a court usher gains admission.

"Her Grace, the Duchess of Bedford presents her compliments, and requests Mrs Ashley to call on her this afternoon."

"What's this about, sir?"

"I don't know, madam. I'll convey your reply to the Duchess."

"Very well, sir. I'll be ready at three if you come back then."

***

"We haven't met before, Mrs Ashley, but I believe you may need some confidential advice on a very important matter. It's about your Lady Elizabeth. She was twelve in September, so the Court is naturally becoming more interested in her future. Can you tell me whether she has started her periods yet?"

"That's a very personal question, madam."

"No, it's certainly not, Mrs Ashley. In her case it's a matter of national importance. And what is your answer?"

"She has not, madam. She is still a child."

"Well, this interview is very timely then. You haven't much experience of the Court, have you? All those country manors for royal children! Quiet backwaters. You don't seem to realise how significant this question is - for our nation and for the King's Grace himself. Unless Lady Bryan explained it to you?"

"Lady Bryan never wanted to discuss politics, madam."

"How wise she was. She is of the nobility, and had lived a long time at Court. She understood all the unwritten rules here. But since she retired, you've had no-one to advise you. In fairness, I suppose your position as Lady Elizabeth's lady mistress was just about acceptable while she was illegitimate. But then, of course,

1

last year His Majesty graciously elevated her to a place in line to the throne. No doubt His Majesty assumed that her entourage from then on would be selected from the nobility. But, in fact, nothing changed! So you, a mere Gentlewoman, have retained your position as head of her Household. Astonishing!".

"With great respect, madam, when Lady Bryan had to leave us, to serve baby Prince Edward, my appointment to take her place was approved by the Court. By Lord Cromwell himself."

"Ah! Lord Cromwell. Another Commoner who rose high at Court. And where did his ambition take him? To the block. The Court can be a dangerous place for newcomers…"

"I am sure, madam, that Lady Elizabeth is content with my care of her."

"Up till now perhaps, Mrs Ashley. But we must look to the future. The near future. I am telling you today that it will be your duty to inform the Queen and the King's Secretary as soon as her periods start. Any delay on your part would be unthinkable. Is that clear?"

"Yes, madam. I suppose it's about the succession, is it?"

"Don't ever say that word again. It's close to treason. Terrifying."

"I'm sorry, madam. I'm out of my depth here."

"Now, finally, how long have you been serving Lady Elizabeth?"

"Nine and a half years, madam."

"Actually, you probably won't be with her much longer. Once her periods start, she will be a fertile royal lady, ready to take her place in the King's plans. That's why we at Court are now interested in her – Sir Thomas Seymour himself was asking me about her just the other day. Her Household then will surely need to be led by well-born ladies. Several ladies, in fact. New positions at Court are always sought after. The Queen herself will probably organise it."

2

"I do hope, madam, I might still be able to serve her in a lesser capacity?"

"I really can't say, Mrs Ashley. Actually, I seem to remember that you yourself got married only a few months ago? You'll surely soon be pregnant and be thankful to leave royal service. So the timing will be most convenient for you. That will be all for now. I have other people to see."

Kat Ashley walks slowly back to Elizabeth's quarters. Her tears well up. She has been like a mother to the girl, and separation would be a terrible shock to both. Elizabeth was devoted to her, and would definitely try to resist it. But Kat knows that her own rank at Court is humble, and she will have to submit to any change without a murmur. Yes, she thinks, it's time I reminded her about periods. And their implications. We'll soon be moving into uncharted territory: here be dragons. But I must try to stay in her Household. She can't forget how resentful Elizabeth had been when she told her she was going to marry John Ashley. She had begged her not to marry, and had sulked for weeks, finally declaring, 'Anyway, Kat, *I* will never marry!'

***

"Well? What was all that about?"

"I can't tell you just now, my dear. Too many servants around. And the King's music master will be here any minute. We'll have a private talk later. When I put you to bed."

"What about?"

"We've got to look ahead more, sweetheart. It's about the future."

"What does that Duchess have to do with our future?"

"Well, nothing personally."

"But you're upset."

"Shh. It will have to wait."

3

***

Later in her bedroom Elizabeth sends out Sally, the nursemaid who sleeps there with her.

"Now, Kat, whatever happened? What did she say?"

"She was just advising me to be prepared for when you grow up, in a year or so. I took it to heart too much, I expect. I don't look ahead enough."

"What do you mean?"

"Well, as you know, when your periods start, you become a young woman. Ready to marry and have children. You'll live here at Court much more – like Lady Mary. You'll have very high rank. Your Household will have to be chosen from the nobility."

"But why are you sad?"

"I'm not from the nobility. So she didn't think I could stay with you then."

"What a nerve! How dare she say that? I'll call her here tomorrow to apologise to you."

"No, please don't do that, my dear. You mustn't make enemies at Court. You'll need all the support you can get here. You see, Lady Mary will always have her uncle, the King of Spain, to watch over her. The Prince of Wales has that powerful Seymour clan. But you're different. You're alone. You haven't got family allies to stand up for you here."

"You're forgetting, Kat! I have the strongest allies of all: the King and Queen!"

"Yes. Look, I mustn't ramble on like this. Careless talk. Keep all this between ourselves, won't you?"

"Alright. But you must tell me if she bullies you again. I won't ever let you leave me."

And she hugs Mrs Ashley close.

"Anyway, Kat, this isn't urgent. Even when my periods start, I won't want to marry for a long time. Lady Mary hasn't married yet. And she's seventeen years older than me. It's like Jacob in

4

the Bible: the older sister has to be married first. I don't know anyone yet I'd like to marry. And I'm sure I wouldn't want to live far away, like Yorkshire or Wales, where I don't know anyone. So that will narrow the field."

HUNSDON HOUSE, HERTS. APRIL 1546

Lady Bryan limps in to the parlour. "Good morning, Kat. I've had a good sleep now, and got over the journey. I'm sorry I couldn't get here in the winter. It takes me a long time to travel these days. But I'm so glad I came."

"It's wonderful to have you back with us, milady. I'm sorry to have asked you to travel. But I'm not allowed to take Elizabeth off this royal estate. I know you understand the rules."

"And where is she now?"

"She's having a riding lesson in the park. She was thrilled to see you yesterday. But I can talk to you more freely now."

"Well, you said in your letter I could help you?"

"The fact is that I need your advice. I didn't like to put it in writing – you were always reminding me to be wary in royal matters. It's about her future. When we were at Court at Christmas, the Duchess of Bedford summoned me, to ask whether Elizabeth had started her periods. She said the whole Court was becoming interested. I would have to inform the Queen as soon as it happened. She warned me that some grand lady would then take over Elizabeth's Household. She was very condescending and superior. She said – rightly – that I don't have enough experience of Court etiquette and procedures. It depressed me a lot. So I thought of you. I've no friends at Court. You always seemed to know everyone."

"It was natural for me. I'd been there for many years. My husband was chamberlain to Queen Catherine – the first Catherine."

5

"That Duchess said Elizabeth would become very important when her periods start. She even hinted at marriage negotiations. Surely Elizabeth would be too young for that?"

"Not if she's royal, I'm afraid."

"Well, what happened with Lady Mary?"

"Her case was quite different: she had a mother! Queen Catherine was most assiduous in supervising Mary's growing up and preparing her for marriage. So I had nothing to do with that."

"But she didn't have to marry very young."

"As it happened, no. The fact was that by the time her periods started, she and her mother were being sidelined. His Grace the King was growing very concerned that he had no sons. He thought it was because he had married his brother's widow. So the Queen and Mary were out of favour, and no grand marriage was planned for Mary."

"But today would she have to marry before Elizabeth?"

"Usually, yes, I think. But she's now thirty. Royal men want a younger bride. For longer fertility. They want male heirs – that's their priority."

"So Elizabeth will be more eligible than Mary. Not what we hoped. But what do you mean by 'royal men'? She won't have to marry abroad?"

"I should think so. That would be expected." She lowers her voice. "You never met Queen Anne did you? She was executed just before you joined us. But I remember she was desperately trying to arrange a betrothal for Elizabeth with a son of the King of France. You see, that would have confirmed that her child was legitimate, and her own marriage was valid. Queen Anne felt very insecure because she hadn't produced a boy. She was frightened she would be divorced, like Queen Catherine. Anyway, it all fell through because the French turned it down. Queen Anne was terribly upset. Elizabeth was only one at the time! Yes, and then when she was four, the King looked into betrothing all three of his children to the Hapsburg royal family in Spain and Germany. So, both her parents were intending a foreign marriage. There's no getting away from it, Kat."

"It's much worse than I thought! She'll hate the idea of leaving England. So would I, of course and what would John say? But I love her so much now. If I was allowed to serve her, I just couldn't stay behind."

"I'm sure, my dear, you'd be allowed to serve her, with all your experience. And from what I know of Elizabeth, she'd certainly have very strong views about that. She's a fighter like her strong-willed parents."

"Yes. But she can't fight the King! I'll have to start alerting her to a foreign marriage." Kat puts her head down in her hands. "I really dread it, milady. She'll hate the idea. You wouldn't be prepared to broach the subject with her, would you?"

"If it helps, I could be there with you when you give her the unwelcome news? You must do the talking, but I could quietly back you up; she's still fond of me, and she'd know we were trying to help her. I mean, we can't change her destiny, but forewarning her will help her adjust to it."

"That's very kind, milady. It would be a great support. I know I mustn't delay. Perhaps tomorrow morning?"

***

The comfortable old nursery at Hunsdon is now used as a day-room for reading, embroidery and music: ladies' pursuits. Mrs Ashley is sitting in a sunny window-seat with Elizabeth as they read the Bible together:

'The Lord's my Shepherd. I shall not want...surely goodness and mercy shall follow me all the days of my life.'

Lady Bryan leaning on her maid's arm comes in and is settled in a chair. Mrs Ashley bobs a curtsey, and the maid leaves.

"Today, Elizabeth" falters Kat, "I must talk to you about the future again. Lady Bryan has been educating me about royal traditions, and it's very important for you to understand."

"You don't look very happy about it. Don't say you can't stay with me!"

She clutches at Mrs Ashley's arm and is enfolded in a hug.

"No, no. Lady Bryan says I wouldn't have to leave your service."

"So much for that know-all Duchess, then."

"Yes, that's the good news. But there is some difficult news. It's about your marriage. I've got to tell you. It's almost certain that you will marry a foreign Prince and live in his country."

"What? Leave England? Forever?"

"I'm afraid it's a long-established pattern for Princesses."

"But that's really frightening". Her eyes fill with tears.

"It's all my fault, my dear. I was too ignorant of royal custom and politics. I should have been teaching you long ago about your future as a Princess. Lady Bryan knows it all, and luckily she has warned me now. I'm so upset. I hate to see you crying."

"My dear Elizabeth", says Lady Bryan, "growing up is hard for girls, especially I'm afraid for royal girls. I'm sorry to be the bearer of upsetting news. But you're a particularly brave girl, and now you'll have some time to get used to the facts. Royal betrothals usually take a long time to organise. And it is a very important role you'll have: making an extra alliance for our great King and country. You would do it so well too. And look how good you are at languages."

"I'll just, just pray for it not to happen", gulped Elizabeth. "I'm so scared."

"Well, I'll be bold enough to say that the real trouble is that you haven't had a mother. There. I knew your mother. Yes, I did. I remember how she tried so hard to betroth you to a French Prince. She spoke excellent French, and she conferred with the French Ambassador about it. You were only a one-year old then. So, you see she was planning for you to marry abroad. But she would have prepared you for it from childhood. I hope that will help reconcile you to accepting it?"

Elizabeth has put her hand over her mouth.

"Yes, I know we mustn't talk about her, but she did want the best for you."

"I don't know anything about her", says Elizabeth, breathing fast, "Except that I mustn't ever mention her. I've had four stepmothers, but I've never lived with them. They never talked about my future."

"That's the trouble, my dear. You weren't really their concern. I'm a very old lady now – seventy-five! – and I'm going home tomorrow. But I've always felt proud of your spirit and courage. I'm quite sure that once you've got over the shock you will rise to this royal challenge. Needs must. Kat will support you. But you have no choice. You are a pawn in this matter, my dear child. Don't let His Majesty detect anything but obedience".

Leaning on the chair arms Lady Bryan gets to her feet. She curtseys to Elizabeth and then gently kisses her hands. "Trust in God, my dear. Shall we read that beautiful old Psalm again that I heard when I came in?"

***

Hatfield House, 20 July 1546

To Her Gracious Majesty, Queen Catherine
   With great respect I write to inform you that the Lady Elizabeth has this week experienced her first monthly period. I was advised last year to notify you when this happened.
   Your humble and obedient servant,
   Mrs Catherine Ashley
   (Lady Mistress to The Lady Elizabeth)

WHITEHALL PALACE, 24 JULY 1546

An usher precedes the Queen and two ladies along the corridor to the King's apartments. Guards open the door to the Anteroom, where Sir Anthony Denny bows before her.

"This audience with His Majesty", she says, "Will be private. Whenever he is ready to receive me. How is he feeling today?"

"No better, I'm afraid, Your Majesty. The ulcers on his leg seem to be worse. Walking is very painful."

"Any further advice from the doctor?"

"He says each case is different, madam. But he expects a full recovery in due course."

"Yes. That's what he told me. Good news, of course, but not very cheering to this sufferer. The King does not take kindly to being restricted in any way."

"His Majesty is still intent on going on his annual summer progress next month, madam. Whether you could bring your influence to bear?"

"No. I'm afraid not."

A bell sounds, and Sir Anthony pulls a heavy curtain aside and opens a door. The Queen walks forward alone and curtseys deeply with bowed head.

"Well, Kate. Another morning, and I'm no better. What the hell's wrong with my doctors? It must be their fault. I was never ill when Butts was my doctor. It's only six months since he died, and I've been suffering all this pain. I sacked Chapman last month, but the new one's just as bad. He looks sick himself, pale and nervous. It's just these damned ulcers. Apart from them I'm in my prime. Nothing wrong with my appetite."

"I pray every day, My Lord, for the cure to come soon."

"It's not right that you can swan about the Palace and do what you like, while I'm stuck here like a prisoner. They showed me a great chair on wheels, but I'm never going to be seen at Court in that contraption."

"My Lord, I have some family news to cheer you. May I dismiss your attendants for a short time?"

The King brusquely waves them away.

"Well, what's this about?"

"It's about The Lady Elizabeth. It's my duty and pleasure to tell you that she has started her monthly periods."

"So. She has grown up then. When did we last meet?"

"She was at Eltham Palace with the Prince of Wales at Easter, My Lord."

"Yes. He was looking quite the young man! I remember thinking she was very thin. No womanly curves then."

"Well, God willing, those will come now."

"Hmm. She won't need curves. Being my daughter is enough to attract suitors. Yes, this is an important development. A useful alliance could be made. My sisters both married kings. Margaret was only fourteen. The first step is a portrait. That's essential; with copies to be sent to foreign Courts. No Holbein now. Who was that fellow who painted you last year? He'd worked with Holbein."

"Master John, My Lord."

"Her dress should have that same wide neckline. The clothes must be very grand, and lots of jewels. That will remind foreign Courts that I've restored her to the succession. Bed-curtains will form the background, to show that she is now marriageable. Yes, I'm right, kings' daughters can actually be useful at this stage. The Seymours won't like her being promoted to the world. But, of course, the Prince will always come first. Very well, Kate. You know what I want. You must commission your Master John."

"Thank you, My Lord."

"And no delays. I shall follow this up. Leave now and send that nurse in."

The steward walks up the wide staircase contentedly; he has been employed at Hatfield for over twelve years. A royal manor, which at intervals houses royal children. After a few months they are moved on to another such place, and Hatfield is cleared, cleaned and waits serenely for the next visit. England is at peace under the Tudors for fifty years now and the old Civil War of the Roses nearly forgotten. There is some religious dissension, but King Henry is strong enough to defy the Pope and establish his new Protestant Church. The steward wouldn't quarrel with that. The country is prospering, and his own job is an enviable one. This morning he's taking last night's post up to the nursery quarters. 'Nursery' is really the wrong name. Lady Elizabeth, who's here now, will soon be thirteen. And the Prince of Wales is nearly nine.

Thank heavens we've got him. We had to wait twenty-eight years for an heir. Long live the King!

A maid takes the letter, and hands it over to Mrs Ashley. She falters as she sees the grand seal.

"What is it?", says Elizabeth.

"It's from the Queen. It must be her answer to mine."

"But it's addressed to me."

"So it is. Would you share it with me in your room?"

Whitehall Palace, 24 July 1546

To Her Grace, The Lady Elizabeth.

Hearing that you have attained womanhood gave me great pleasure. I informed The King's Grace, who is most gratified. He looks ahead to achieve an important marriage alliance, which would benefit his people. As a first step His Majesty has commanded me to engage a portrait painter to celebrate your adulthood. The portrait (and copies of it) would be circulated to Courts in Europe, to advertise that you are now eligible for marriage.

His Majesty has chosen the fine painter, Master John, who painted me last year. He will be available whenever we are ready. The King has stipulated that you should wear very grand clothes and jewels for this important portrait. That will underline your royal status. You will need to come to London to help me choose the fabrics, and be fitted. Jewels can be lent from the Royal Collection. Master John can then start the portrait!

The King does not want any delay to this project, so I require you to come to Whitehall Palace next week. For myself it will be a happy opportunity to see you again.

Catherine, The Queen.

"Oh no! It's all happening too fast. If it was just the Queen, I might stall her a bit. But the King himself! I daren't. No-one dares. It's all such a shock."

She slumps down on her bed, sobbing, and clutches Kat, who puts her arms round the girl, and gently rocks her to and fro. "Oh Kat! I feel so worried. Usually I can't wait to get to London. To dress up and be at Court. But not this time. My life has always been in these dear old royal manors. With my faithful servants. Perhaps I'll be kept in London now till I have to marry? Will I ever see Hatfield again? Or Hunsdon or Ashridge? I don't feel grown up at all. If I have to live abroad, I'll have to start my life all over again. As a foreigner cut off from my own people." She buries her face in her hands. "I can't think of any way out. Unless an English Duke applied to marry me?"

"But no-one would dare. It would be seen as setting his cap

13

too high." Kat lowers her voice, "Do you remember The Exeter Conspiracy? I'll say no more.

Now, my dear. We've just got to face the fact that this happy old set-up of ours is coming to an end. We must obey the summons. I'll have to order a ten-guard escort for three days' time, and we'll stay a night at Enfield as usual. First we must compose a reply to the Queen."

***

Hatfield House, 28 July 1546

To her most gracious Majesty, Queen Catherine

Dear Madam,

I was most honoured to receive your letter. Thank you for your kind interest in my future. I have only just become an adult, so I will much appreciate your guidance and support.

Please convey to the King's Grace my humble thanks for commissioning a portrait of me.

I have made arrangements to travel to Whitehall Palace next week, as you require.

Your humble and respectful step-daughter,
The Lady Elizabeth

WHITEHALL PALACE, 1 AUGUST 1546

The Lady Elizabeth in a dark court dress and her hair loose is escorted by two Ladies in Waiting to see the Queen. She gives two deep curtseys when she enters the Presence Chamber.

The Queen in an elegant taffeta dress and her hair held back in a golden net, glides forward. She lifts Elizabeth's hands in her own and kisses her forehead.

"My dear, welcome to Court. I'm always so glad to see you when you visit London. And now that you're grown-up, I hope that you'll be spending more time at Court. In fact, I've decided that you will be top of my own list of ladies in waiting whenever you are here! From now on, you see, you'll be the third lady at Court."

"That's a great honour, Your Majesty."

"Of course: but it's also your birthright, as the King's daughter."

"I'll try to be worthy of it, Ma'am."

"I know you will. You're a very dedicated character."

"My education has been very good, Ma'am, but I don't know much about procedures at Court."

"That is a good reason why you need to spend more time here now. Because most of your future life will revolve round the Court. Probably a foreign Court! I hope you will make many good friends, but you must always be aware of your royal status." She laughs. "I've had a steep learning curve in that myself! Although I am the First Lady, I have no royal blood. I'm only Queen because His Majesty generously raised me to this high rank. I try to learn from the King what I should say and do."

"Then I will try to learn it from you."

"Well, I know what the King wants us to do now. He wants us to produce a portrait of you. And it will indeed be grand. You will have to look like the royalty you are. So I have tailors ready to sew, and the artist waiting for my summons. First, you and I must choose the design and a rich fabric. My own dressmaker will come here this afternoon with designs and samples. It's a most exciting project, isn't it?"

"Thank you for all your trouble, ma'am."

"But you don't look as thrilled as I'd hoped?"

"I'm very sorry, ma'am. Please forgive me. I feel I'm swept up in a whirlwind."

The Queen puts an arm around Elizabeth's shoulder.

"Yes, it has been a rush, my dear. You see, once His Majesty has decided on something, he expects his wishes to be fulfilled very quickly. Rightly so, of course. 'Le roi le veult'. But don't worry. You will feel better when you see the new respect shown to you at Court – now that you are grown-up! Come back this afternoon, and I will show you the fabrics and designs."

***

The Mistress of the Robes is with the Queen this afternoon. She leads in a smart gentleman who carries a sheaf of dress designs. He spreads them on a table, and the Queen beckons Elizabeth over.

"Have you seen my recent portrait hanging now in the great Hall?"

"Yes, ma'am. It's beautiful."

"Well, the King has admired it too. And the one detail he mentioned for your portrait dress is that its neckline should be the same as mine. That is a low, square neckline, almost off-the-shoulder. It will be most attractive to men! So it will add to your charms in the eyes of suitors. In my case, of course, there was no question of any man making advances to me. But the King, I believe, wanted to show the world what an elegant, up-to-date Queen he had chosen. I wouldn't claim that myself, but, of course, the King does have impeccable taste."

"I liked the fur over-sleeves."

"They were so warm! But mine was a winter portrait. Well, we've got three designs here with the wide, square neckline. Which do you like best?"

"I will defer to you, please, ma'am."

"In that case, let's have this one with its wide overskirt. Now we will see the cloth merchant."

Another gentleman is shown in and makes a deep bow to the

Queen, and another to Elizabeth. Two assistants follow, pulling a trolley loaded with rich fabrics. All sorts of dazzling silks and satins. The Queen advises Elizabeth to have bright colours, to emphasise her youth. Together they choose a brocade heavily embossed with gold (reserved for the royal family) to be the underskirt and undersleeves. Then a rich scarlet damask as the final layer. In spite of the girl's fears, she can't help feeling excited at this lavish parade.

"And the neckline must be studded with pearls", the Queen says, "A matching French hood must be made too. And I will take you to the Jewel House, to select some Royal jewellery – a girdle, necklaces and rings." She laughs, "It's quite a treat for me to dress you up. I think Master John will paint you in the same pose as my portrait: standing and holding a prayer-book. But your picture will have bed-curtains as the background, because it's a betrothal image."

Elizabeth's fears re-surface. But she can't express them. She knows the Queen has no power, for all her elegant clothes. It is dawning on her that royal females have no say in their own future.

"I am very young to be betrothed, ma'am."

"But it's because you're so important now. When I told the King your news, he said, 'Royal daughters can actually be quite useful at this stage. My father,' he said, 'arranged my sister Margaret's marriage to the King of Scotland when she was fourteen'. So there you are. I can see it's all come as a shock to you, my dear. I can't help feeling you should have been brought up in the knowledge of your likely future. If only you'd had -. Well, no more to be said. What a lot of progress we've made today."

THE STABLE COURTYARD AT WHITEHALL PALACE, 4 AUGUST 1546

Sir Thomas Seymour meets an old friend.

"Hello there, Sir John! Haven't seen you for ages."

"No, Sir, I've not long been back at Court. My father died, and I've had to see to our estates in Northampton."

"Sorry to hear that. Have you time for a stroll in the gardens, before I go home?"

"Of course. Lead on."

"I was just checking on my horses. Tomorrow morning I'm heading to Hertford Castle to visit my royal nephew. Ned and I like to keep in good touch with him."

"That's a long ride."

"It's nothing to me. I always beat Ned to it when we set out together. Even though he has a far better horse!"

"How is the Prince? He never seems to come to London."

"No. He's a fine, strong lad, thank God! But the King doesn't want him to run any risk of journeys, crowds, pestilence or fevers in the big City. Though he was at Eltham Palace at Easter. And he sometimes gets to Windsor, so the King visits him there. He calls him 'England's Treasure', which is surely true."

"Indeed."

"Ned didn't want me to visit our Prince of Wales, you know. He wanted to be the only uncle. He's always been jealous of me. But I wasn't going to be pushed around. A boy needs two uncles. Jane would have wanted me to keep an eye on her son – I was certainly her favourite. Anyway, Ned has inherited all our father's estates at Wolf Hall and elsewhere, so he should leave the Prince to me."

"Well, it's wonderful to hear first-hand that the Prince is thriving. And I hear that The Lady Elizabeth has come to Court?

I've glimpsed her in the past at Easters and Christmases."

"We've all done that. But this is different. Word is that she's now grown up. Marriageable. She'll live at Court a lot more."

"That's good. We need some more young life at Court."

"Amen to that (between you and me). But I doubt she'll be here for the long term. I hear the King has called for a grand portrait of her. The Queen has been ordering rich fabrics and jewels for it."

"You hear a lot."

"The Court grapevine doesn't miss much."

"So, what does this portrait mean?"

"Sounds to me like a betrothal picture. It will be shown to Ambassadors here, and perhaps carted round abroad. It's the marriage market."

"She's rather young."

"Not for a Princess. Anyway, the negotiations can take a long time. Not just finding a useful Prince, but a dowry to be agreed. A Treaty to be signed. France and Spain wouldn't have her. It would have to be a Protestant. German States? Sweden?"

"So, what do you think of her being promoted in this way? It's not long since she was just a bastard."

Tom laughs. "Ned doesn't like it! But it doesn't matter what I think. I'm the King's loyal servant. I keep my mouth shut."

THE KING'S COUNCIL CHAMBER, WHITEHALL PALACE, 6 AUGUST 1546

The King is sitting on a throne at the head of the table, as Sir Anthony leads in the other eight Councillors.

"Be seated. Gentlemen. Before you consider the new revenues needed for the defence of Calais, I have an announcement to make. My daughter, Elizabeth, has recently come of age to be married. Yes, it is good news. I intend to seek a royal betrothal for her abroad to benefit my country. You all have useful contact here with Ambassadors, so you will be able to make enquiries about potential candidates. Let Denny know as soon as possible of any suitable leads and the reactions of the Ambassadors. Remember I am keen to get this project under way very soon. Meanwhile, I have arranged to have a grand portrait of her painted by Master John. In due course it could be displayed round the relevant Courts of Europe."

Archbishop Cranmer stands up and bows.

"Yes, Thomas?"

"Your Majesty. With your permission I would like to say a few words about the Lady Elizabeth. As her godfather, I am probably the Councillor here who knows her best. I can assure the Council that she is a most Christian, accomplished and intelligent young lady, who will grace any Court she lives at. She is a great credit to His Majesty, her father. My fellow-Councillors may quote my words to the Ambassadors."

"Well said, Thomas. A pleasing finale to this main item on our agenda. You may leave me now, Gentlemen. Return at two o'clock to discuss the defence of Calais. I shall not be with you then. But I will expect to receive the result of your deliberations. More tax revenues are essential for Calais."

The Councillors, seemingly unperturbed, rise and file out of the Chamber. Denny remains behind, and summons three groomsmen to help the King to get to his feet and walk in some pain slowly back to his Privy Chamber.

THE KING'S PRIVY CHAMBER,
6 AUGUST 1546

"The Queen has arrived, Your Majesty, in response to your summons."

"Bring her in. Now, Kate, it's high time I heard what progress you've made with the Elizabeth project. I've just told the Privy Council about it."

"It is my top priority, Your Majesty. Her Grace arrived here six days ago. I interviewed her the next day, and together we chose a design and fabrics for the portrait dress. It's now being made up by a fast team of my best seamstresses. It will be ready in three days' time. I will then take her to the Jewel House to select a necklace, girdle, and rings. I do hope that meets your expectations, My Lord?"

"Satisfactory so far, I suppose."

"Perhaps, My Lord, would you then do her the great honour of granting her an audience here in her splendid outfit? I sense she is quite nervous about her future. She would gain a lot of confidence from your approval."

"Yes. I think I should see her. I know Cranmer thinks highly of her. Of course, I haven't had the time to get to know her. But now that she's grown up, she'll be more important at Court – sit with us on the High Table at feasts etcetera. So, at last, I'll have a chance to assess her."

"Her Grace will be very grateful to come into your presence, My Lord. She knows you have always watched over her devotedly and provided the Royal Manors and her servants. She has wonderful memories of meeting you at Easters and Christmases all her life. And then three years ago, of course, she came to our private wedding ceremony, along with Lady Mary."

"Oh yes. Does Mary know about Elizabeth and the betrothal portrait?"

"Not from me. But she's always well informed. Usually by the Spanish Ambassador, I believe."

"No surprise there, then".

"May I venture to offer a thought here, My Lord?"

The King grunts.

"Well, I've always been touched, and a little surprised, that Lady Mary is very fond of Lady Elizabeth. She's seventeen years older, but they lived together for several years, and she has shown great affection towards her. But now I'm afraid that, when she comes back to Court, she might resent Lady Elizabeth getting a lot of attention here. Of course, Lady Mary will always have the seniority."

"Mary has no right to be jealous! You ought to know that! It's entirely her own doing that she's not married. She insists on the old religion, and only wants a Spaniard. But I promised King François that I would never have an alliance with Spain. I can't overrule Mary, because she has very powerful relatives. It's maddening that I can't command my own daughter. Anyway, where is she now?"

"She's gone to visit her estates in East Anglia on a summer visit, My Lord."

"I don't like that. Her presence gives tacit encouragement to all the dissidents there. Such as the Duke of Norfolk. And his son. At least I can command Elizabeth. Let Denny know as soon as the dress is finished, and bring her to see me."

"Thank you very much, My Lord."

THE KING'S PRIVY CHAMBER, 10 AUGUST 1546

The Queen ushers Elizabeth, in her scarlet portrait dress, into the room, and they give deep curtseys.

When they rise, the seated King gives an exclamation, "Oh! Yes. For a moment - in that French hood.... A trick of the light. Yes. What a splendid dress! Such a bright colour. It's all dazzling. Very appropriate for a daughter of mine. And what does my daughter think of it, eh?"

"It is all I could wish for, Your Majesty. And I humbly thank you for this great honour".

"Good. You can be sure I am working hard to secure you an important future."

Elizabeth curtseys again. "I saw Cranmer recently, Elizabeth, and he was praising you."

"The Archbishop has been a most faithful godfather to me, Your Majesty."

"Archbishops have a lot more time than Kings. And now that painter must stir his stumps. He's all lined up, isn't he, Kate? Keep the pressure on him. I might even look in on one of the sittings. Kate – you may stay and play for me now."

Elizabeth backs out of the Chamber with relief. The Queen's Lady-in-Waiting curtseys to her and summons the escorting ushers and guards. The small procession takes a long route back to Elizabeth's quarters, so that the many Courtiers see her in her finery, and bow their heads as she passes.

"Welcome back! Did it go well? Tell me about it soon. The seamstresses are here waiting to undo that dress and take it to the royal wardrobe."

The three seamstresses come forward with curtseys and gather round the silent Elizabeth, removing the jewels and French hood first. Then they unhook the wide oversleeves, and the undersleeves, the two skirts, the bodice and the undershirt. They wrap the costume in fine linen, and leave the room.

Elizabeth slumps down on a chair and sobs, "Oh, Kat, I just want to get home to Hatfield!"

"So do I!"

"But I'm stuck here for now. My audience with the King went smoothly, thank goodness. My heart was beating so fast. He liked my dress. But he's pressing ahead with the painting. He's quite impatient about it. So I can't see any hope of escaping a foreign marriage. I feel like a prisoner. What can I do? I'll just keep begging God to avert it all. Everyone bows to me here now, but what's the good of that when I won't be in England much longer? I'll soon be long gone and forgotten."

Kat sits beside her and puts a sturdy arm around her shaking shoulders. "I'll be there with you, sweetheart. Let's try to have some hope. At least you'll always have a palace and servants. It will be an exalted position. And His Majesty will protect you wherever you live. No son-in-law would dare to cross the King of England! Can you imagine it?"

A Lady-in Waiting arrives, and curtseys to her. "The Queen has sent me, Your Grace. I am her sister, Lady Anne Herbert. The painter will see you this afternoon in the special quiet room set aside for royal portraits. He has the instructions for the background, and will need to see you there, wearing the dress. He'll work out the composition and make a preliminary sketch. I believe you have been painted before?"

"Yes. Twice. About three years ago a small silhouette of my head. Edward and Mary had the same. Then, last year, Mary and I were painted at either side of a large picture with the King and Prince Edward in the centre. But we were only very minor figures at the edges of the painting. And our likenesses weren't good."

"Well, you'll certainly be the only person holding the stage in this portrait! And close up too."

"Can I - I would like Mrs Ashley to come with me."

"Well, Your Grace, the Queen deputed me to be your chaperone for these sittings. But I don't see why there can't be two chaperones. All the better, surely? I'll send the seamstresses up with the dress, and I'll come back for you at two o'clock."

WHITEHALL PALACE, MASTER JOHN'S STUDIO, 11 AUGUST 1546

Meister Johannes sits on the window-seat in the studio, waiting for Elizabeth. He knows the room well, and likes the large north-facing windows; they give good light, without the distraction of shifting sunshine. He looks over at the palace roofs, and down to the courtyards and the Thames. Plenty of merchant ships, some from Germany. He feels a twinge of homesickness. But he's making good money in London, and has a queue of commissions now. He's had to postpone them for this new one. Now he begins to hear the tramp of the escort guards coming up the stone stairs, and he stands up and pulls his brown painting smock straight around his shoulders.

"Enter, please".

He makes a deep bow to the slim young girl in the dazzling dress who leads the way into the room. The elegant Lady Anne follows her, and says, "This, Your Grace, is Master John, the celebrated portraitist".

Another woman, perhaps a lady's maid, in a plain linen dress and cap, also comes in, and the guard captain closes the door and leaves them.

"And this", says Elizabeth, "Is Mrs Ashley, my Lady Mistress."

Master John gives a lesser bow. "Good Afternoon, Princess. For me it is a great pride to paint you. You ladies must sit down there. But the Princess must stand in her beautiful costume. I make a quick drawing today. The plan is simple: a dark background and this bookstand with a Holy Bible. The Princess will hold a prayer-book. The Queen instructs me so. I see the dress is very bright. That is good. It shows an important person. But in a portrait the sitter's face must always be the most bright. It is Summer, so the light is good for me. Princess, did you hear the name, 'Mr Holbein'?"

"Yes, of course."

"I helped him in his workshop. And sometimes in this same studio. He trained me. We both came from Germany. He painted King Henry in here, and Queen Jane, and Prince Edward. And I believe earlier he once drew a portrait – "

"Master John!", calls Lady Anne, "Stop there! Remember what the Queen told you."

"Ah, yes. Pardon me….Anyway, Mr Holbein has started to paint Princess Mary, but the poor man fell ill suddenly, and died three years since. Then I was commanded to take up his brushes and finish that portrait. Later I painted this Queen, and the King liked it. So here I am today to paint you. So I have royal experience; you can trust in me. How is the King, by the way?"

A pause, then Lady Anne says, "We don't ask that question, Master John. The King is always well."

"Good, good. Now, Princess, come and stand here. Listen carefully. This only takes one hour today. Then for three days I paint only the background. After that, you must come back for the portrait. After I paint your head and shoulders, you need not come every day. The costume is very elaborate, but I can place this dress on a tailor's dummy, to save your time. Then my good assistant, Wilhelm, helps me paint the dress. It probably takes me about six weeks in all. Now I am beginning. You Ladies may do your needlework."

THE COURTYARD AT WHITEHALL
PALACE, 17 AUGUST 1546

Tom Seymour hurries across.

"Good morning, Lady Anne."

"Sir Thomas."

"We go back a long way, don't we?"

She nods, slowly.

"And how is Her Majesty?"

"Very well indeed. Enough said."

"May I also enquire then about our newcomer at Court, the Lady Elizabeth? I've seen you escorting her to the portrait studio. What are your impressions?"

"Good impressions. She is very young still, of course, and not used to being the focus of attention. But underneath the reserve and courtesy, I sense courage and determination. A growing awareness of her status."

"Not much joie de vivre perhaps?"

"Perhaps not, at the moment. She's anxious about her possible future life, in a foreign marriage."

"So, she won't adorn our Court for very long?"

"It's no secret that this portrait will be an advertisement for betrothal. And a foreign prince is the norm," and she turns away.

"Just one more question, Lady Anne? Who is the woman who goes with you to the studio?"

"Mrs Ashley, Elizabeth's governess."

"Court rumour has it that she's naïve and indiscreet...?"

"All I know is that Elizabeth is devoted to her. No more questions. I'm on my way now to another sitting, so you must excuse me."

He gives an extravagant bow and watches her enter the Palace.

There's a tug on his sleeve, "A word with you please, Sir Thomas."

"Ah, my dear Duchess. At your service."

"I wanted to let you know that my daughter, Dorothy, is now seventeen and coming to stay at Court. The Duke and I hope to arrange a suitable match for her soon. Now that you are back from defending our Channel, I wonder whether you may be looking for a wife at last? It's unusual to remain so long a most eligible bachelor?"

"Alas yes, madam. I am nearing forty – middle-age has arrived. But, as you know, I am only a younger son. Ned is the lucky man who has inherited our family money and lands. Plus, of course, the grand titles: 'Viscount Beauchamp' when Jane married the King. 'Earl of Hertford' when Prince Edward was born. *To him that hath shall be given*. Yes, Ned was able to marry early, and has two sons by now. As for me, I need to find a very rich heiress – a lady with no brothers – to maintain my way of life. So I must decline your kind offer."

"I must look elsewhere then. You have my sympathy, Sir. Everyone remembers how unlucky you were a few months ago, when the Duke of Norfolk himself offered his daughter to you in marriage. You must have felt very proud. But then her brother, young Surrey, set his face against it, and Norfolk caved in to him. What a disappointment! But I do hope you are on good terms with your brother?"

"We have certain interests in common. Family connections. I am sure I don't need to spell it out to you, Madam. You keep yourself very well informed, don't you?"

The ancient oak woods and pasture lands look tired in the late Summer sun. The grass is yellowing, and the oak foliage is dark rather than green. This old royal hunting ground has seen most of the kings of England, and the current one has enjoyed it more than most in his long reign of thirty-seven years. He's not here today, but about twenty of his smart younger courtiers are gathering. Their grooms are leading fine horses out of the stables, and helping their masters to mount. They ride slowly around, mingling and waiting for the Master of the Hounds to sound his horn.

The Earl of Hertford seeks out his brother. "A word in your ear, Tom."

"At your service, Lord Ned."

"Keep your voice down. It's about the Prince of Wales and his future. Let's ride round that oak."

"So?"

"He may have a change of scene on the horizon. Of course, he doesn't come to London, but he needs to be near it. And we should be ready to seize the opportunity. Whenever it arises."

"Some might want to hold him back."

"But we would stand by him. Be prepared. No division between us on this, eh Tom?"

"Agreed."

"That's enough now. I can see Surrey is watching us."

"That arrogant boy. Norfolk has spoilt him – a cocksure eldest son! So proud of his noble lineage."

"Remember: this chat has been about our horses and the Hunt."

"And, no doubt, our late-lamented sister, Queen Jane."

"Exactly. And, one more thing, Tom – I've noticed that several top noblemen have been showing me more deference recently. They're trying to ingratiate themselves. Do you find the same?"

"Why would they bother? I'm not a nobleman, am I?"

"For God's sake, Tom! Take that chip off your shoulder. We're both Seymours."

They turn their horses sharply and move apart to join the other huntsmen.

MASTER JOHN'S STUDIO, WHITEHALL PALACE, 19 AUGUST 1546

"We meet again, my three grand ladies. Yes, I have better chairs for you this time, Lady Anne. Make yourselves comfortable. You see the background now on the canvas? Next, is the most important stage of my painting. I must capture the likeness of the young Princess. I have to paint her face. So many people in the world, but each one has a different face. That is how we recognise each other, isn't it? That is the true test of the portrait artist. Faces are unique, and I must capture this one.

Now, Princess, you are at a mystery age. You are not any more a child, but not fully adult. You are on the doorstep of adult life. So I must catch that too. It will probably take me four or five days. Because it's not good if you become tired or bored. So you cannot stand here for very long at one time. I can only paint your face when you are alert and comfortable. You have a sensitive look and I must do justice to that. I think you are also a cautious person. You don't speak much. Is that right? I want to know the character of my sitters. You should look at me, but I cannot keep talking with you, because I have to concentrate hard on my work. Perhaps Lady Anne or Mrs Ashton could read to you a bit? Thank you. So, let us begin. May God be with us, and good health to the King!"

"Master John!"

"Ah. Pardon, Lady Anne, pardon. You see, in Germany we always say that. When I say goodbye to a friend or a shop-keeper, that is what we say. It is good wishes."

"Well, here in England in 1546 it is very unwise to say it. The Queen hopes to look in on us in a day or two, so watch your tongue."

ELIZABETH'S QUARTERS, WHITEHALL PALACE, LATER THAT DAY

Elizabeth waits impatiently as the three dressmakers carefully untie the various pieces of the beautiful costume, and hang them up in a large cupboard. When they leave, she bursts out, "Did you hear, Kat? He said it would only take him four days to paint my face. After that, he and Wilhelm will paint those grand clothes, but I don't have to be there. Do you think we could go home to Hatfield or Hunsdon then? I hate being in London, all these hot Summer days. It's lonely. I hoped I'd at least see Harry and Cathy here. But he's away on an embassy and Cathy's expecting another baby in October, so she's gone back to Rotherfield. I just want to escape."

"Amen to that! I'm a nobody here. John enjoys all the company and chat, but I'm such a country girl. I hate being stared at. But I've noticed that you seem to enjoy it."

"Yes, I don't mind the stares. They remind me that I'm royal now. I acknowledge them by a small lift of my hand. Anyway, I think I'll have to pluck up courage and ask the Queen. She was the one who summoned me. She can always order me back when I'm needed here. I'll tell Lady Anne to get me an appointment with her."

"Lady Anne is quite bossy, my dear."

"I know. But I'm the third lady in the land now…"

THE QUEEN'S APARTMENT, WHITEHALL PALACE, 25 AUGUST 1546

Elizabeth is shown in to the Queen's privy chamber, and gives a deep curtsey. The Queen takes Elizabeth's hand.

"How lovely to see you again. I was so delighted to see how the portrait is developing. I told the King all about it. Sadly, that studio is so high up that he can't reach it as yet…But I hear you have a request for me?"

"I do have a great favour to ask, Your Majesty. It's that now Master John doesn't need me for three weeks, I'm full of hope that you might allow me to return to Hatfield for a bit? I would so like to go back to the countryside and my own Household, please? And I miss my riding so much. I don't really know anyone here."

"Well. I can understand that you are still very fond of the Royal Manors where you've grown up. Of course, the King would have to decide. One thing is that your thirteenth birthday is coming up, and I've been planning a grand celebration in the Great Hall here. So you would have to be back at Court by 5th September. But that would give you a week at Hatfield, wouldn't it? Leave it with me. It's his decision, as always."

WHITEHALL PALACE, THE QUEEN'S APARTMENT, 26 AUGUST 1546

L ady Anne steers The Lady Elizabeth through the audience chamber into the Privy Chamber. Elizabeth drops her deep curtsey and raises hopeful eyes to the Queen's.

"No, not Hatfield, my dear."

Elizabeth can't stop her tears welling up.

"We all have to accept the King's will", the Queen says gently. "We mustn't question it. His Majesty, I gather, did not have time to get to know you much while you were a child. But, now that you have become an adult, he hopes to see more of you. He does you the honour of expecting you to be at Court far more. He wants you to experience appearing at public functions, along with Lady Mary. This is the time to establish your adult status in the eyes of the Court and the country."

Elizabeth nods with bent head, and the Queen pauses.

"You see, we need you to buttress the Royal Family. Both the King's sisters have died now, and they left no sons, so there aren't many of us. And, of course, the Prince of Wales never comes to Court. You will also be helping me to try to stand in for His Majesty until his leg ulcers are quite healed."

"Thank you, ma'am."

"Good! Think of it as all part of your training for your new grown-up world."

"I'll always do my best to help you, ma'am."

The Queen puts an arm round her and draws her to a chair next to her own.

"Meanwhile, my dear, you may join me and my Ladies for our needlework sessions. And I'll arrange special music and dancing lessons for you, while we wait for our Master John."

***

Whitehall Palace, 29 August 1546

To His Royal Highness the Prince of Wales, at Enfield Manor

My dear brother,

I hope you are in good health. I am sad that we have not been together since Easter. I have kept hoping that our Households would be united again, but it has not happened. We have spent six happy childhood years together, and two more seeing each other regularly. I shall always be thankful for that. But now our futures are destined to be apart. So I want to explain it to you.

As you see from the superscription, I am now at Court. I was summoned here by Their Majesties because I have recently become of marriageable age. I now know that Kings' daughters are expected to marry foreign princes and live abroad. You can imagine that I was very unhappy to learn that, because I love my homeland so much. The King's Grace has ordered a portrait of me in a very grand costume. Copies will be made and taken to foreign courts to attract suitable Princes. And then I will have to depart – perhaps for ever. I will be very homesick. I just hope that Kat and Sally can come with me; and maybe some other English ladies too.

Meanwhile, you will certainly spend the rest of your life here in England. I hope you may find time to write to me, as I will surely do to you. It will help me to bear my exile.

My thirteenth birthday will be celebrated here on 7 September. The Queen has graciously arranged a grand dinner, but I know you must guard your health and stay away from London. I wonder where your birthday on 12 October will be spent? Perhaps at Hatfield. I don't know

35

if I would be allowed to visit you then, but I will ask the Queen. She is kind to me. One of my earliest memories is your Christening at Hampton Court nine years ago. I was just four, and your uncle, Sir Edward Seymour, carried me in the procession. And I remember curtseying to your mother, Queen Jane. She was wrapped up in warm furs.

I hope, dear Edward, that your studies are going well. Please remember me to Master Ascham. I confess that I envy you your riding and archery practice. I can't do that here in London, and I dream of our country Manors.

I pray every day for your health and happiness, and that we may meet again very soon.

Your most respectful and loving sister,
Elizabeth

***

Enfield Manor, 4 September 1546

Dear Elizabeth,

Thank you for your letter. I was very sorry to hear that you will have to live abroad before long. I will miss you a lot. Lady Mary is twenty years older than me, so you are my closest sister. I have no-one closer. Because I hardly ever see Their Majesties. But I am sure it is your duty to marry whichever prince is chosen by our gracious King and father. Your prince will be lucky to have you. And you will be serving England by making an alliance with a foreign country.

Master Ascham was interested to hear your news. He thinks highly of you. I love riding and hope one day to enjoy hunting like the King. When I'm older, I will ride out with him. I'm getting better at archery too.

I wish you a happy Birthday. I hope you can come to my Birthday.

May God be with you, my dear sister.

Edward

LADY MARY'S ROOMS AT WHITEHALL PALACE, 6 SEPTEMBER 1546

A guard escorts Lady Elizabeth and Lady Herbert into the salon. They both make deep curtseys to Lady Mary, as she sits on a tall chair, scrutinising Elizabeth.

"Good Day, Elizabeth."

"Good Day, madam", and Elizabeth smiles happily as she looks up.

"We haven't met since Easter, and I wanted to see you before your formal Birthday Feast tomorrow."

"Thank you, madam."

"You may leave us, Lady Herbert. The Queen has told me about your grand portrait, Elizabeth. I gather the Royal Jewel House lent you many treasures."

"Her Majesty arranged everything, Mary."

"And she tells me it is a betrothal portrait. To show you off to foreign courts. No doubt you're proud of that?"

"Well. Just to you, Mary, I'm very sad. I don't want to be sent abroad. I'm too young. I'd be very homesick."

Mary nods slowly. "To me you still look very young. Though you have grown taller. I hear that the whole Court is focused on your future now. When I was thirteen, in 1529, no fuss was made of me. Sadly by then your mother had usurped the King's affections. Later, he bitterly regretted that, of course. But it certainly blighted my own young adulthood."

Elizabeth hangs her head.

"If your scandalous mother had not bewitched the King, I would have married a Spanish King. I was already betrothed to him. But once my legitimacy was questioned, I had no suitors. And now, seventeen long years later, I won't marry anyone but a Spaniard. In honour of my dear mother. I want you to know all this from me now you have grown up."

Silence. Then a small voice, "I'm sorry about the past, Mary."

"Don't think I'm blaming you for it. That would be unjust. But I can never forgive your mother. She betrayed the King with many lovers, you know. She had a fair Trial, and was beheaded for her sins. But you know all that."

"I don't remember her. I've been told a bit, but I mustn't talk about her."

"I trust in God. He will recompense me and my mother. If not in this world, then in the next. Well, we lived together your first 3 years. I was deeply unhappy at that time. But you were a merry little soul, and actually cheered my spirits then. I've kept an eye on your progress ever since. You were always a quick learner. And later very good at Latin and other languages. What about your religious instruction?"

"I read the Bible a lot, madam."

"In English or Latin?"

"In both, madam. I go to chapel on Sundays, wherever I am. And Archbishop Cranmer occasionally teaches me."

"You've never known the Catholic faith in which I was raised. We seem to be divided on that all-important subject."

"I hope you can still be my friend, Mary?"

"I'll continue to keep a close eye on your development. But as you're to marry abroad, we won't know each other well. I presume you will be sent to Sweden or one of the little German states. Quite a comedown. The larger Catholic countries who are faithful to the Pope would not want you.

To them, of course, you are a bastard and heretic. But I will pray for your soul."

"Thank you, madam".

"You may go now. Enjoy your big day tomorrow. Once you're abroad, the Court will soon lose interest."

Elizabeth curtseys deeply, and backs quickly out of the salon with bent head.

THE GREAT HALL AT WHITEHALL PALACE, 7 SEPTEMBER 1546, NOON

The King and Queen sit on thrones on the raised dais at the head of the long banqueting table. Lady Elizabeth wearing her portrait costume stands between the King and the Archbishop, and Lady Mary stands next to the Queen. They watch as Courtiers and Officials file in to take their places, while minstrels play in the Gallery. There is a murmur of appreciation and relief at this rare appearance of the King. Then two Heralds sound a fanfare and command everyone to sit down.

"Pray silence for His Grace the King!"

The King remains seated but his voice is strong.

"My subjects. Today is the thirteenth birthday of my younger daughter, The Lady Elizabeth." He takes her hand. "I now present her to you all. This banquet is to celebrate her reaching adulthood. I am proud of my daughter, and will seek to choose a foreign prince for her, to make an alliance for England. Now stand, and pay homage."

The room rises and gracefully bends in bows and curtseys.

"You have all acknowledged Elizabeth's high rank in my Court. Now the banquet in her honour may begin."

Elizabeth suddenly kneels beside her father and kisses his hand, an impulsive gesture applauded by the Queen and Courtiers.

The Archbishop raises a hand. "Your Majesty, we thank you for this happy celebration. We wish every blessing upon The Lady Elizabeth. For what we are about to receive, may the Lord make us truly thankful. Amen."

***

After the cheerful feasting, Sir Anthony Denny gives a vote of thanks to the King and asks the Courtiers to file out of the Hall, and leave His Majesty with his family. The Queen then asks the King's permission to take the five royal ladies (for there were no males) into the adjoining Parlour. She kisses the King's hand, and leads them away. Sir Anthony then summons the King's team of strong groomsmen to help support his huge weight slowly up the stairway behind the throne to his private quarters.

In the Parlour the Queen, in order of precedence, allocates chairs to Lady Mary, Lady Elizabeth, Anne of Cleves, and the King's two nieces, Lady Margaret Douglas and Lady Frances Brandon.

"I thought this was a good moment for you all to meet our dear Lady Elizabeth, now that she's reached adulthood, and will be at Court more.'

"Welcome to Court, madam", says Lady Margaret warmly, with a curtsey. "What a glorious dress! Frances and I know Lady Mary very well, because we're all about the same age. But now we can get to know you too!"

"Yes, madam," says Frances, "I've seen you at Christmas and Easter in the past, but of course you were still a child then. I've got three younger daughters of my own who perhaps could be friends for you one day."

"Thank you, Frances, I'd like that."

Anne of Cleves comes forward with a curtsey, and Margaret and Frances turn away to talk to Mary.

"So, here is my other stepdaughter! When we first met I could hardly speak any English. But that is six years and eight months ago. It's so good to see a fresh young face at Court. But I hear that you may not wait long? One talks of you marrying abroad, like I did. Yes? What a shock it was for me. New language, new customs – so different from all I'd known. But don't worry, my dear, you're much younger than I was, so you'll learn very fast. We Princesses have to go where we're sent, is it not? My brother sent me here, and your father will send you. You should know that, even though my marriage was short, King Henry gives me a lot of money. And he gives me a new name: The King's Sister. So I am in the Royal Family. In the middle. I must curtsey to you and Mary, but Margaret and Frances over there must curtsey to me. And he gives me Hever Castle and Richmond Palace, where I usually live. But I had to promise I will not return to Cleves, which does upset me. So: 'Here I stand, I can no other', as the great Luther said. But", turning to the Queen, "I'm worried about the King. I am not here for some months, and now I see he is bad at walking, and terribly fat. Whatever is the matter?"

Silence falls in the room. Then the Queen says carefully, "The King has been suffering with painful leg ulcers, and the Doctors have been slow to help. But I'm glad to say that he now seems to be recovering. In fact he has just agreed that from now on he will take part again in many engagements in the Palace reception rooms. He will use a special chair on wheels, so that his leg ulcers will be able to rest and heal. This will complete his recovery. So, no need for any alarm, sister Anne."

"Well, God be thanked. That is good news. After all, England needs many years for the little Prince to grow up."

"I'm sure, Sister Anne, all of us in this room should know not to hint at the succession. Don't refer to it again, and don't let your Ladies at Richmond gossip".

"I'm sorry, Your Majesty. I'm afraid I don't always understand secret English customs. But I must now get back to my Richmond Castle. My boat will be expecting me. We must catch the tide. Thank you, Your Majesty for the grand banquet. And I hope, Elizabeth, you will come to visit me at Richmond one day before you leave England. Perhaps I will teach you some German? I will write to my brother, the King, and ask him, for your visit."

Elizabeth looks at the Queen, who nods slowly.

"Remember, you are my family now. We are six ladies and the little Prince. Goodbye, everyone. God bless you all.", and with a deep curtsey Anne leaves the Palace.

"She must be lonely sometimes," says Margaret, "It's sad, but she doesn't really belong here. She doesn't fit in, does she? She's never learnt music or dancing or card games, let alone archery. All she can do is needlework!"

"She has a good heart," says the Queen, "She can't help her upbringing. I find her a very direct person."

"The King has certainly been most generous to her," says Lady Mary, "In spite of her admiration for Luther. When I was young, the King published a condemnation of Luther's heresies. And I can't help begrudging her Richmond. It's so modern and comfortable. I used to stay there often. So did you, Elizabeth."

The ladies turn their focus on to Lady Elizabeth, to get to know this newcomer. They question her about her pastimes and her studies and about the little-known Prince of Wales, whose Household she often shares.

"How old were you when you married?" she asks Frances.

"I was fifteen, madam. My parents chose Lord Grey for me. I wasn't important enough for a foreign prince."

"What about you, Margaret?"

"I only married last year. I was 29. It was a very late marriage." She glances at the Queen. "I had better say now that – to my shame – I also had two secret engagements. When I was 20 the King found out Thomas Howard and I were privately betrothed. He was, rightly, very angry, and sent us both to the Tower. I was terrified, but after a few months the King, in his great mercy, released me. You won't believe my stupidity, but a similar situation happened when I was 24. My dear mother (who was here then) was furious, but I know she pleaded with the King to forgive me, and for her sake he did. So, don't ever try to follow your heart and deceive our noble King."

"A very cautionary tale indeed", says the Queen, "But Elizabeth is a prudent girl and would never encourage a secret suitor."

EARL OF HERTFORD'S LONDON HOUSE, 7 SEPTEMBER 1546

"Well, Ned, so we've witnessed the promotion of Elizabeth. Soon to go overseas, more's the pity. Hail and farewell, little Elizabeth. What does this mean for us Seymours?"

"On the face of it, nothing."

"And behind the face of it?"

"Time will tell. If she has sons, and our protégé doesn't, we Seymours could lose out."

"Have you written off Lady Mary? I bet that banquet put her nose out of joint. She was looking inscrutable, as usual."

"I don't write anyone off, Tom, I try not to make aspersions."

"'Aspersions', eh? And did you see Norfolk? Not happy. Elizabeth seems to have broken ranks and squeezed Mary out."

"Well, that's the King's doing. 'Le roi le veult'. End of story."

"Unlike you, my Lord, I have a living to make. I keep an eye on people with power, to see where my future may lie. So, I also noticed Dudley eyeing up Elizabeth. He's got five sons, you know."

"He'd be mad to suggest such a thing, and you're mad to mention it."

"Where will she end up? Hanover? Denmark? Sweden? Hesse? Nowhere very powerful. Not worthy of her, I reckon. She's an attractive girl too. Quite a catch!"

"Whoa, Tom! I'll forget that. Thin ice there."

"I can't help champing at the bit sometimes. I'm always being held back. It's not my nature to be patient."

"If we can hold our course steadily, we may not have long to wait."

"You said it. Better go now."

And Tom stands up, and strides out into the London night.

MASTER JOHN'S STUDIO, WHITEHALL PALACE, 9 SEPTEMBER 1546

"So, Princess. Here we are again, for your last few sittings. Wilhelm and I have been working hard on the costume." He folds back a screen to reveal the painting on his easel, and there is a satisfying gentle gasp.

It is a dramatic revelation. The bright figure of Elizabeth leaps out of the subdued background of dark curtains. Every detail of the elaborate costume is now painted. Her hands over the skirt are still to be added, and some finishing touches to the face and hair.

"Master John, you are making a wonderful picture. I think I look older there than I feel. But I can't help being very proud of it."

"I will advise Her Majesty to come and see it tomorrow. She will be thrilled with this", says Lady Anne, "She has been under constant pressure from the King on this matter."

"Thank you, ladies. We are all happy! I must say now that only the King himself could have commissioned such a portrait. It reminds me of the one Master Holbein painted of Prince Edward when he was only one-year old. All in scarlet and gold, like this portrait. It is clearly royal.

And now I take up my brushes again, to work on the hands. And something also: I think I will need only two more sittings after this one. Then two weeks of first drying time, before I can take it to the King. After that it will need another month to dry out completely. Stand here again, Princess, and hold this prayer book of Cranmer in your hands. Just so."

LADY ELIZABETH'S QUARTERS, LATER THAT DAY

"Thank you, Ladies, bring the costume back in the morning. There will only be two more days in the studio. After that you must preserve the dress carefully in the Royal Wardrobe. It might be needed at Christmas, I suppose, before she grows out of it!"

"Oh, Kat. I'm exhausted. It's not the actual sittings -or should I say 'standings'? It's all the pressure of being at Court, and my timetable rushing on. The portrait is marvellous, but we know what it means. I'm just being swept along. I'll soon be swept right away from England." She clutches Kat's hand. "I'm only a puppet paraded in the costume. A tailor's dummy."

"We've got to be realistic, my dear. I can't think of anything that could stop it. But we'll be together. And it will be months, or even years, away."

"I must get back to Hatfield soon. I'll ask the Queen if I might leave Court, once the King has approved the portrait. Then I could have a quiet time with my own Household till Christmas. I'm so longing for home."

"Me too. I can never quite relax here. I wasn't made for Court."

THE KING'S ANTECHAMBER, 1 OCTOBER 1546

Master John and Wilhelm are setting up their tall easel opposite the two thrones. They fix the portrait on it and drape a large cloth over the front. Wilhelm is then dismissed, and the Queen enters with her sister and Lady Elizabeth. They remain standing, while Sir Anthony goes through to the Privy Chamber to request the King's presence.

His Majesty, helped by two groomsmen, limps in and sits heavily on the larger throne. Master John bows and the ladies give deep curtseys. The King waves the ladies to their seats. "I've had to wait for this painting. At last it's here, so let's waste no more time. Let it be revealed."

All eyes are on the King, as Master John carefully unveils his painting to a brief, tense silence.

"What an impressive portrait! It demands an audience. It will catch attention wherever it hangs. It will fulfil my purposes. I like the way you've suggested her coming bosom with that slight shading. Well done, Master John."

"Thank you, Your Majesty. You have a very fine daughter here, is it not?"

"Er, yes. Of course, I have given her every advantage."

The smiling Queen says, "My Lord, Master John has explained to us that the portrait will now need to finish drying for a month in the studio. After that final stage it must be framed and displayed to Ambassadors."

"So be it. If that delay is necessary. Don't forget that copies must be made of it, to be taken abroad in due course."

THE QUEEN'S PRIVY CHAMBER, 3 OCTOBER

Lady Elizabeth answers the Queen's summons, and again looks up hopefully from her curtsey.

"This time, my dear, the King's Grace has given permission for you to leave Court for the moment. Yes! Mercifully, he has been in better spirits since viewing your portrait. It has been a very satisfying project for him to have. Also, he has received a letter from the Prince of Wales asking if his sisters might join him at Hatfield for his birthday celebration on the 12th of October. The King himself would like to have attended too, of course, but he's not quite ready to travel that far yet. And he can't spare me. Lady Mary will attend for just two nights. But you may stay on there with Edward in your old style, merged Households for at least a month. It's convenient and economical for you both to share Hatfield Manor at present. You may travel there with Lady Mary on the 10th of October, with one night at Enfield Manor on the way. I will arrange the escort, and send the orders to Enfield and Hatfield."

"Thank you very much, Your Majesty. I'm so happy. Thank you for all your help and kindness."

"My sister, Lady Anne, will accompany you. She will be a chaperone of suitable rank, now that you are an adult. Yes, Mrs Ashley will remain as a member of your Household. Heaven forbid there should be any whisper of scandal, like the last wretched Queen invited. I have to take my responsibility for your well-being very seriously.

I'll miss you, Elizabeth. I've enjoyed our portrait project, and the King has given it his stamp of approval – not easily won. So, it's been a great success. Enjoy Hatfield again, but keep an inward eye on your future path, won't you? Your life in the Royal Manors will soon be ending", and she gives Elizabeth her hand to kiss.

THE GREAT HALL AT HATFIELD, 12 OCTOBER 1546

Some important guests are assembling, to wait for the Prince of Wales to join them for his ninth Birthday feast. The Lady Mary, Archbishop Cranmer and the Duke of Norfolk are his godparents. With them are the Lady Elizabeth and the Seymour siblings (Edward, Tom and Elizabeth). The Prince's half-sisters each have a Lady-in-Waiting, and guards stand to attention round the room. Sir Richard Page, Controller of the Prince's Household, consults his seating plan. In order of rank he escorts each guest to their seats on the High Table on the dais. Lady Mary followed by Lady Elizabeth take their places on either side of the Prince's throne. The Archbishop is put next to Elizabeth and the Duke of Norfolk to Mary. Then on Mary's side Edward Seymour and Elizabeth Cromwell (née Seymour). Next to the Archbishop is Tom Seymour. Sir Richard leaves to attend to the Prince. The scene is set, and all eyes are on the door behind the throne.

They all stand and bow their heads, as the Prince comes in. He's slim, growing taller and has a cheerful confidence and clear voice.

"Thank you for coming to my birthday party. I like seeing so many of my relations here. Especially my sisters! The King's Grace can't come, because he has too much work in London. When I'm older I'll help him with his work. He sent me a new horse. God save the King!"

Everyone claps, and he sits down happily.

Archbishop Cranmer raises a stately hand, and says, "Thank you, your Royal Highness, for inviting us all today. May God's blessing be upon you for a long, healthy and Christian life. As His Majesty has often remarked, you are the most precious jewel in this realm."

Sir Richard sounds a large gong, and a troop of servants comes down the hall bringing food and wine to the High Table at the far end.

HATFIELD, 13 OCTOBER 1546

Early next morning the Seymour brothers set off back to London, starting together to have a private talk.

"Well, that was a bit of politicking, Ned. Circling each other and seeing how the land lies, eh? Everyone looking ahead, and seeking alliances perhaps. Where will the power lie?"

"Not all the power-players were here. John Dudley and William Paget, for two, didn't qualify for this select party. Dudley's very ambitious, but we may need him. Anthony Denny can never leave the King's side. Bishop Gardiner, Mary's friend, couldn't get an invitation either. But Norfolk will keep him informed."

"The King's always suspicious of conclaves of his noblemen.

But he does allow it to happen for his son's birthday. He wouldn't choose Norfolk as a godfather today, though"

"No, but Norfolk is a very careful old hand, Tom. He wouldn't step out of line. But he does need to rein in that arrogant son of his. He calls us 'upstarts'!"

"Yes, I'm watching that chancer."

"It takes one to know one."

"Chancers sometimes win, you know."

"Not in 1546."

"So, what did you make of the sisters?"

"Anne says Lady Mary is ruffled by Elizabeth's recent emergence. To Mary, Elizabeth is a bastard who shouldn't be royal. And her youth shows up Mary's age. But Mary's used to being patient. She knows that Elizabeth will be off-stage before long, married to a foreign prince. I don't know what Mary thinks about the King's health; she must see that he's getting worse. Elizabeth hardly knows him yet, so she hasn't really noticed the deterioration."

"Did you see how well she gets on with the Prince? They were chatting and giggling away all through the feast. But usually she seems quite a cool customer now. Very deferential to the Prince and Mary, but suddenly aware of her own high status. Quick to pull rank at Court."

"Has she snubbed you then, Tom?"

"Not yet. We Seymours are a bit of a grey area to her, because she knows we're so close to the Prince."

"We've got to keep close to our Prince. The future is at stake now. And the timing of it. It's obviously getting nearer. So keep your ear to the ground. As soon as it happens, I'll ride North to escort him to London, and you must try to counter any plot to seize power. Look at the last boy-king. He was soon in the Tower."

"I know the stakes, Ned. We're together in this at least."

HATFIELD HOUSE, COURTYARD,
13 OCTOBER 1546

"I'm sorry you've got to go so soon, Mary. I don't see my family much."

"Thank you, Your Grace. I'm sorry too. But I have duties at Court. The King and Queen will be expecting me to give a full account of your Birthday. They are so proud of you. I can report how much you've grown, and how healthy you are. Your future is often in my thoughts these days. Remember, I'll always support you. And I do hope that your religious education is in good hands out here?"

"Oh yes, my chaplain is very nice. He plays catch with me too. I often beat him at catch."

"Well, please keep me in your prayers, and I will certainly keep up my prayers for your soul. Listen to God, and follow His true path. God bless you, my dear Prince." She hugs him, then gives a deep curtsey, and walks away towards her horse, her Lady-in-Waiting, the armed escort and London.

THE OLD NURSERY, HATFIELD,
13 OCTOBER 1546

Roger Ascham strides in to join his friends, Kat and John Ashley.

"Well, they've all gone! How marvellous to be together again. I feel quite a hermit out here since Easter. Bring me up to date with all the London news. I do miss all the talk. Where's Lady Anne, by the way?"

"She's gone out on the riding lesson with the children. She has to chaperone Elizabeth quite closely now, though I still do most of the indoor care."

"I suspect that she doesn't really want to be here?"

"She did protest a bit. There's no-one else of her rank here. But the Queen laid it on the line. She was told she could be replaced after Christmas. She does know Elizabeth quite well now because of the portrait sittings."

"Oh yes, I heard about that."

"Well it's an amazing painting but a betrothal portrait. The King commissioned it to mark her adulthood. Lady Anne was appointed to chaperone her while we were at Court. She did lend status to Elizabeth because I haven't any to give her!"

Ascham laughs, "You've given her everything else, Kat."

"Well, I've enjoyed nearly all of it, but not going to Court! It's such a relief to be back here, isn't it, John?"

"Absolutely. Did you hear, it's no secret now, the King can hardly walk? He uses a special chair on wheels, which his groomsmen push to meetings and dinners."

"Really? Very demeaning for him."

"Must be. It doesn't improve his temper. The Court's in a strange, tense mood. A lot of questions in the air, but no-one dares voice them. It wouldn't suit you, Roger, with your enquiring mind."

"Hmm. Well, in that case it's some more country living for me. I'm a town mouse at heart, but I am very fond of the little Prince. I do see the Seymour brothers; they take it in turns to visit him every month. They like the hunting here too. Dutiful uncles. But tell me more about Elizabeth, such an intelligent girl. The Prince showed me her sad letter. I helped him draft a reply."

"Right. Yes, she's still devastated about her future. The King intends copies of the portrait to be displayed at Protestant Courts, to forge a new alliance. She's struggling to accept the idea. But of course, she can't protest."

"And what about you?"

"I couldn't abandon her now. And dear John says he'd come too, at least some of the time. I don't think our French or Italian will be any use – let alone Latin! Do you know Germany at all?"

"Not yet. But their religion suits my thinking. And they have brilliant painters. I'll pay you a visit!"

"We'll hold you to that," says John. "They make good beer and wine too."

"And how long are you here for?"

"Till Christmas, anyway", says Kat. "After that, I suppose Elizabeth might have to stay at Court for a formal betrothal, or interviews with Ambassadors. We go where we're sent! I so hope some delays can be built in for her."

"We'll have to make the most of you, then. The hunting season's upon us, John, so we'll get some fantastic riding – much better than Whitehall, eh?"

"Wonderful! Just what I need. I don't have much of a role here, so I've lots of free time. Perhaps you can make an archer of me too?"

"The Prince's lessons have to be fitted in somehow! Though, actually he enjoys archery too now. He was most impressed that I'd written a book about it."

"So were we", says Kat, "and the King himself asked for a copy last year."

"Don't sound so surprised", laughs Ascham. "It's high-quality stuff. But it was a labour of love, in between my Latin and Greek lessons. You should try writing, John. You said you'll have time on your hands. Something about horses perhaps? The printing-presses have been a godsend for authors."

"Mm. I'll bear it in mind. I could start some jottings about riding. To be continued in Germany, perhaps?"

"Of course! I'll expect to see it on my visit. In fact, you must call it 'The Art of Riding' and dedicate it to me!"

***

Hatfield House, 30 October 1546

To Lady Catherine Knollys, Greys Court, Rotherfield Greys, Oxfordshire.

Dear Cathy,

I heard yesterday from Sir Francis that your baby arrived safely on 17 October. I was so relieved! I like the name Edward. Your third son and fifth child in six and a half years! I hope you and the baby are still safe and well. No wonder we don't meet often enough these days!

I last saw you at Harry's wedding in May, but I like it best when you come and stay with me in the country sometimes. But I'm afraid those happy visits are now over. The reason is that my periods started this summer, and I suddenly found that I'm expected to marry some foreign Prince, and live abroad. It was a great shock and has made me very sad.

His Grace the King commissioned a grand portrait of me wearing a beautiful red and gold dress and lots of jewels. It will be sent round foreign Courts to attract suitors, and the King will choose the best one. I have no say in the matter. I pray all the time that it won't happen. But I have to hide my true feelings. It's known all over Court now, so Francis may have told you already?

I just want you to know how sad I'll be to leave England and not to see you or Harry any more. I've known you all my life, and you've been my great friends, as well as my cousins. Please pray for me, and keep writing.

May God preserve you and your family.

Your very loving cousin,

Elizabeth

***

Greys Court, Oxfordshire, 10 November 1546
To Her Grace, The Lady Elizabeth.

My dear cousin,

I was so pleased to get your kind letter. Yes, thanks be to God, baby Edward is thriving with his wet-nurse, and I am regaining my strength. We shall be here now for the Winter. Parliament won't be sitting, so Francis doesn't need to be in London.

We shall come to London again in the spring, and I so much hope to find you still there. Francis had told me about your betrothal portrait. It's very hard for you, my dear, to be sent abroad. I'd be frightened, if I had to live abroad. But I'm such a home-body now, with all my children here. Your life is still before you, and you're a brave, confident person. I think you should look on this as a sign of the great pride that the King has in you now. And once you have children of your own, you'll be so happy in your new home. Trust me!

And don't forget that Harry often goes abroad on embassies now. Wherever you live, I'm sure he'll manage to visit you sometimes! We were so pleased you came to his wedding in May – the last time we three Boleyns met.

When you are married, please write to me, and I will always respond.

Give my best wishes to Kat.
My prayers will go with you.
Your respectful and loving cousin,
Cathy Knollys

WHITEHALL PALACE, THE KING'S PRIVY CHAMBER, 10 NOVEMBER 1546

"Well? Speak up!"

"My Lord, I'm pleased to tell you that the portrait of The Lady Elizabeth is now completely dry, and has been framed in the gold frame you chose. It is now locked in the Studio awaiting your orders."

"At last. We must put it to work. Lay on a small Reception for the relevant Ambassadors when it can be displayed. Next week. Tell Master John to produce the little copies, to be sent to our own ambassadors abroad."

"It will be a grand finale to this great project, My Lord. You have achieved it, in spite of the pain you've been suffering."

"The damned pain is only one burden. Far worse is the fear of traitors at Court. I can't be at the centre so much. To dominate it. I have a great instinct for plots, and my suspicions are never wrong. Cromwell was skilled at sniffing out traitors, but he's long gone. It was Norfolk who overthrew him. A King must always protect his throne from usurpers and conspiracies. My spies don't help me enough. Denny is not spymaster material like Cromwell was."

"You have kept this Kingdom safe these thirty-seven years, My Lord, and surely many more to come."

"I will strike them down, wherever they hide." He pounds the table.

THE EARL OF HERTFORD'S HOUSE, LONDON, 12 NOVEMBER 1546

John Dudley joins the Seymour brothers. "Gentlemen. I won't keep you long. I'm sure you agree that we seem well poised. But the handover needs to be quick and smooth with no opposition. I can think of only one person who might wrest control from us: the premier Duke of the realm. He and his ancestors have always been a power behind the throne. He expects a large slice of power as a right. I think you'll agree that he daren't make a move during this reign. But as soon as it ends, he might be planning to seize the Prince, and get rid of us. Don't forget how he brought down Cromwell. We can't risk being supplanted. No mercy would be shown."

"Attack is the best form of defence", says Tom, "I've always known that. I'm for a pre-emptive strike."

"We must move the Prince", says Edward, "Hatfield isn't fortified enough. He needs to be in Hertford Castle for the next few months. He's often on the move. But the King has to give his assent. I'll have a word with Denny."

"Good. Meanwhile we three must watch and listen for any hint of disloyalty by the Duke or his son that we could pass on. I must leave now. God save the King!"

THE KING'S ANTECHAMBER,
14 NOVEMBER 1546

"The next item, Your Majesty, concerns The Prince of Wales. The Lady Elizabeth is sharing his Household at present, but she will be returning to Court from Hatfield this week in response to your summons to attend her portrait reception with the ambassadors. So, with your permission, it seems a convenient time for the Prince of Wales' Household also to move on from Hatfield, to allow for the thorough cleaning and re-stocking of that establishment. Hertford Castle is in readiness to receive His Grace again, with your approval?"

"He doesn't seem to have been at Hatfield long? But his health comes first. And it's a short journey. So I permit the move. I've spent a lot of money on that castle, Denny, and it's very comfortable now. I must inspect it again soon. Put it in the diary for the Spring. The roads will be better then, and so will I."

THE QUEEN'S PRIVY CHAMBER,
16 NOVEMBER 1546

The Queen embraces her sister, "Ah! My dear Anne. Welcome back to Court. You don't know how good it feels to have my own real family with me. You and William are so dear to me. I hope Hatfield wasn't too dreary for you?"

"I did feel a bit cut off. But at least I'm back where I belong for the moment. An unexpected break! Actually, the Ashleys and the tutors there are well-educated company, and of course I've got to know Elizabeth much better."

"Good. How do you find her? I hope she's now reconciled to her foreign marriage?"

"I don't think 'reconciled' is the word yet. She wouldn't make any public resistance. But if there was any way out, I'm sure she would grasp it. And give thanks to God."

"Hmm. Believe me, I do sympathise. But at least she's now had several months to adjust to the idea. She may well be fourteen by the time it's all signed and sealed. I was fourteen at my first marriage. And what's the Prince of Wales like?"

"He's very advanced, I'd say. He's had the best tutors. In himself he's courteous and friendly. Perhaps a bit lonely. My Harry likes friends to play with! I must say he loves Elizabeth. Neither of them has ever really had a mother or normal family life."

"I'd like to have been more of a mother to him, like I was to my earlier stepchildren. But I hardly ever see him. Anyway, thank you for going to Hatfield. Now I've had to call Elizabeth back for this ambassadors' reception tomorrow. I've had a smart Court dress made for her, along with these jewels. Take them to her, so that she can have a dress rehearsal today. And remind her that ambassadors are the representatives of foreign kings, so she'll need to curtsey to them. Escort her to the audience chamber just before noon. The King and I will be there, and the ambassadors will soon follow. They'll want to talk to her a bit, but it won't take long. It will be a very low-key affair now."

ELIZABETH'S QUARTERS, WHITEHALL PALACE, 17 NOVEMBER 1546

"Take heart, my dear. You look so elegant; that dark red and black sets off your fair skin. And velvet is always warm. Bring over the head-dress, Sally. There. A French hood is really pretty, isn't it? It's a frame for your lovely auburn hair too. Look in the mirror."

"I wish you could come with me to these grand occasions."

"Ah, rank is everything here specially when the King himself is present. But I'd love to be a fly on the wall, and admire you."

"Whenever I'm with the King I have to be very brave. I know he watches me closely, and I mustn't let him down. But it's a great strain not to tremble or stammer."

"If it was me, I'd be very jittery. But he *is* your father, my dear, and he's surely proud of you. Oh? That must be Lady Anne and the escort. Good luck then!"

THE ANTECHAMBER, WHITEHALL PALACE, 17 NOVEMBER 1546

Elizabeth and Lady Anne hear the King shouting, as they reach the private entrance.

"It's simply not good enough, Kate! Not for November. I must have more light on the painting. More candles at once, Denny. Guards must hold them next to the painting. Get on with it!"

Elizabeth pauses for a minute or two, then quietly enters with an extra deep curtsey and downcast eyes.

"Rise, Elizabeth. Sit there. I'm trying to display your portrait to its best advantage, but I'm being thwarted on all sides. I shouldn't have to attend to these details at the last minute. It's exhausting."

The King looks flushed and the Queen pale. Servants run in with more candles for the guards, and the portrait on its stand becomes the focus of the room. The main doors are opened for the eight or so ambassadors to file in.

"Welcome, Your Excellencies. I have invited you to this Reception to present you to my daughter here, The Lady Elizabeth."

They all bow and Elizabeth curtseys.

"I am looking to arrange a foreign marriage for her, and to that end I have commissioned the portrait you see there by Master John. It is an admirable painting, and Master John is standing beside it to answer any questions. He has made small copies of it for you to send to your rulers. It will interest all those nations which seek a stronger alliance with England. I will assess any offers for my daughter's hand in marriage, and negotiations for terms and a dowry would follow. Enjoy the wine which is now being served, and make yourselves known to Lady Elizabeth."

Sir Anthony Denny brings forward the Swedish ambassador.

"Good day, your Grace. My country is far away, but twice as big as England. We follow the reformed religion, like you. You would be the first English Princess to come to Sweden. But we do have two princes of about your age. They will be very interested to see your portrait."

"Thank you, your Excellency."

"The ambassador from Frankfurt, Madam."

"Good afternoon, your Grace. My country is a small nation, but very prosperous. We would be glad to have a strong alliance with England now to keep the Pope at bay."

"May I ask a question, Sir?"

"Of course, Princess."

"Do you have music and dancing at your Court?"

"Yes, Madam, we enjoy music and dancing. We are Lutherans but not puritans! Does that meet with your approval?"

"Yes, thank you, Sir."

"The ambassador from Hanover, madam."

"Delighted to meet you, Princess. Tell me what is the book you are holding in the portrait?"

"It is our new prayer book by Archbishop Cranmer, Sir."

"Good. And do you know the Archbishop?"

"Yes, he is my kind godfather, Sir. He helps me with my religious studies."

"And what else have you studied?"

"Italian, Latin, French, music, law and hand-writing."

"You are very well educated, Madam. What about your leisure time?"

"I do needlework and horse-riding, Sir."

"Both together?"

"No!" she laughs.

"The ambassador from Denmark, your Grace."

"May I ask, Sir, what pastimes I would have at your Court?"

"Well, Milady, that would depend on what your husband permitted, of course. The universal rule. But I venture to say that embroidery is always acceptable."

And so the ambassadors filed on; a few words with Elizabeth, then comments to the King.

"Your Majesty, I congratulate you on her education."

"My Duke will be very interested in this proposition."

"A great ornament to your Court."

Finally there is a vote of thanks to the King for his hospitality, for the impressive portrait, and for the chance to meet his charming daughter.

Sir Anthony hands out the small copies of the painting, and leads the ambassadors out.

"Well, Elizabeth, I heard satisfactory reports of you. I think we can expect much interest to be shown in your future. I have set up this project for you, and we now have all the preliminaries in place. There will probably be great competition to secure you, because England is a powerful ally to have. You can rest assured that a Prince will be found. Now tell me how the Prince of Wales is."

"He is very well, Your Majesty. He loves the horse you sent him for his birthday. He's an excellent rider."

"Just like his father!"

RICHMOND PARK,
28 NOVEMBER 1546

John Dudley rides between the Seymour brothers.

"A dark afternoon, Gentlemen. But I have exciting news. Surrey has given us just the weapon to use against him. Yes! Have you heard of his new Coat of Arms? Believe it or not, he has included the Arms of King Edward III. That's a claim to royal descent. The one thing King Henry can't stand. Remember the Duke of Buckingham? He claimed descent from Edward III. Beheaded for treason in 1521. Accused of believing that he would succeed to the throne, and of plotting to kill the King. A good omen for us, eh?"

"We must seize on this, Ned. For God's sake, no more drifting".

"You think it's enough, Dudley?"

"Definitely. The King's more reclusive now. So, he broods more. Obsessive about his throne. His rages are fed by fear. He'll pounce on any threat to the Succession. He won't need much convincing."

"You're right there. He's already full of suspicions. And, if there's any counter-attack, the Prince is now safely in Hertford

Castle. So we must put this to the King at once. I'll get an appointment for the two of us from Denny."

"You aren't leaving me out, Ned? I've as much right to see him as you."

"I'm an Earl and Dudley is Admiral of the Fleet. Our status qualifies us."

"So I'm of no account?"

"Also, also, Tom, you're not the King's favourite courtier. Remember your earlier friendship with the Queen? And your subsequent removal from London to guard the Channel? Keep yourself safe."

"Wise words, Hertford. And, by the way, I'm being tailed by spies of Norfolk's. I imagine you two are as well. So word will soon get back to him about our supposedly secret meeting here. We need to see the King before he does."

THE KING'S PRIVATE ANTECHAMBER, WHITEHALL PALACE, 1 DECEMBER 1546

"People are clamouring to see me all the time. I alone choose who I will see. Denny just puts the names before me. You two are on my Council, so I see enough of you already. Don't presume to think you have a right to private audiences too."

"Your Majesty, we hope you will absolve us when you hear our urgent concerns. We act out of fear for Your Majesty's own safety."

"How's that?"

"It has come to our attention, Your Majesty, that the Earl of Surrey has re-designed his Coat of Arms. He now includes the

Royal Arms of King Edward III. We thought it our duty to -"

"What? How dare he? Good God, that's treason itself! Pitting himself against the House of Tudor. Where is he? Has he raised an army?"

"We don't know any more, Your Majesty."

"This is just what I've been expecting. Evil traitors plotting against me. Call the Commander of the Guard. Make out an arrest order, Denny. Now! And warn the Constable of The Tower. It's an open and shut case. Betraying his King and country. Not a word of this must get out, until he's in the Tower. And where is Cromwell when I need him? The best servant I ever had. It was those Howards who had him beheaded. His spies were everywhere. Now I have to do all his work as well as my own. It exhausts me." He gives several rasping breaths. "No more words. I want action. You know what to do."

***

Enfield Manor, 1 December 1546

To His Grace the Prince of Wales at Hertford Castle

My dear brother,

I hope you are very well. I know we were both disappointed to be plucked from Hatfield so soon. And even more unhappy to be separated again. We'd only been at Hatfield for about six weeks. In the past we used to stay together for several months at each manor. I was not satisfied with the reasons given for this change, either. Sometimes I feel I'm a tennis-ball, batted to and fro from Court to the manors! In fact, a crumb of comfort for the miserable prospect of my coming exile from England is that I'll have a settled home.

But we know that His Majesty has our best interests at heart. I hear he is recovering from the swelling on his legs. I'm told he is gaining strength daily. He graciously presided at my meeting with the Ambassadors. He asked after you, and was delighted to hear of your talent for riding.

Please give my regards to your uncles. Kat is a great admirer of your dashing Sir Thomas, but John doesn't approve!

I miss you, dear Edward, and I miss Dr Ascham and his lively lessons. I shall cling to the hope that we shall all meet again as a family for Christmas at Greenwich. Meanwhile, I will pray for you every day.

Your respectful and devoted sister,
Elizabeth

THE KING'S PRIVY CHAMBER, EVENING OF 5 DECEMBER 1546

Three groomsmen are helping the King to transfer from his chair to his bed, when he suddenly vomits and collapses to the floor, unconscious. Sir Anthony has been dismissed for the night. One of the grooms runs off to fetch him and the doctor. He knows he must not use an Usher, or word will spread. Their rooms, prudently, are not far off. By the time they arrive, the King is semi-conscious and mouthing strange sounds. The doctor checks his pulse, and helps the grooms heave him onto the bed. He grips the King's left hand, and feels an answering clasp; but the right hand and arm have no power or motion. "It's a seizure. An affliction of age. Speech is often affected. Many people recover from a first seizure. But it's very serious. Only time will tell. I will bind his right arm with a warm poultice, to waken the muscles. Keep the fire well stoked this cold night. I will, of course, stay with His Majesty and these good grooms. Seizures are always sudden, and they can often be fatal. I wonder if the Queen should be told, Sir Anthony?"

"I'd been thinking of that. If it was earlier in the day, I would certainly do so. But at this hour it would be better for her to get a good night's sleep. She'll then cope better with tomorrow. The King now seems oblivious to our presence, and it would be wrong to wake him. A question for you, doctor, is should I summon the Archbishop in the morning?"

"Yes. Send a boat early. Extreme Unction may be called for."

THE KING'S PRIVY CHAMBER, 7AM, 6 DECEMBER 1546

"His Majesty has survived the night, Archbishop, which is a good sign. You must understand that his right arm is still inert, and his speech can't be understood. But he recognises us. So his mind is functioning."

"Thank you, Doctor. Your Majesty, I am here to humbly bring you religious comfort and support in this hour of need. May I kneel at your bedside and say some prayers? Thank you. Almighty God, Father of all Mercies, look upon thy faithful servant Henry Tudor as he suffers from this sickness. He has always led a Christian life, and he even established a new national Church here to the glory of thy name. We remember how thy Son, our Lord Jesus Christ, healed the sick many times during His life on earth. We pray that for His sake thou wilt restore our King to good health, and will continue to watch over him all the days of his life. We thank thee, God, for our creation and preservation through all the perils of this earthly life. And we look for the resurrection of the dead and the life of the world to come. We ask this not trusting in our own righteousness, but in thy manifold and great mercies.

Your Majesty, may the Lord bless and keep you. May he lift up the light of his countenance upon you and bring you his peace, now and forever. In the name of the Father, the Son, and the Holy Spirit, Amen. May I now anoint you, Your Majesty, with some holy oil, to sanctify your body and soul?"

The King nods, and grips the Archbishop's hand. He struggles to speak, and tears come to his eyes.

"I will leave you now, Your Majesty, in the care of these good doctors". He presses the King's hand. "I'll continue to pray for you, and will come back later, to see if you want my company again."

He backs out of the bedroom, and sinks into a chair. "What a shock, Sir Anthony. He looks so pathetic lying there helpless, like a beached whale. Our country is in great peril. I doubt if we can stop word getting out?"

"No. Not now. I've been fighting a rearguard action for some months to fend off rumours about the King's health. But the Court is bound to hear of his collapse now. On a personal level I'm sure your visit has soothed him. You've served him a long time, haven't you?"

"Yes. I do seem to have stayed the course longer than many others who were close to him."

"Please don't leave the palace for the next few days. I shall need you. I must now bring the Queen into this. The King will surely be expecting to see her soon, so for her own sake she needs to know. I'll break the news to her."

THE KING'S PRIVY CHAMBER, 9AM, 6 DECEMBER 1546

"Your Majesty, the Queen is waiting to see you. May I show her in?"

The King nods, and gasps and the words, 'Yes, yes' emerge.

"His very first words, ma'am!"

"My Lord – what a hopeful sign!"

"I, I, I….", he shakes his head impatiently.

"My Lord, may I sit here and hold your poor hand? The doctors tell me that rubbing it gently may help to stir it back to life. What a terrible shock you've had. But words are coming back. Something in your throat must be blocking them. But they are finding a way through. Keep calm, My Lord, and trust in God."

"But I must get, get… I can't…."

"Well done indeed. You are saying more. Shall I play to you now, My Lord? Something peaceful and calming? The doctors say you should rest. Bring me my lute."

THE KING'S ANTECHAMBER, 9.30AM, 6 DECEMBER 1546

"He's asleep now. I feel worn out too. I'm afraid I can't face the Court today, Sir Anthony. After all these months of assuring them that the King's health is nothing to worry about, I wouldn't carry much conviction, would I? But I think a special meeting of The Council would offer some confidence that the situation is under control. Do you agree? They won't all be here, but it would give a semblance of normality."

"I'll summon as many as I can straightaway, Ma'am. Perhaps Cranmer, as he's here, would be Chairman. Anything is better than inaction and a limbo".

"It buys us a little time. But even if the King recovers quickly, the future will be changed. The country will need definite plans for future stability."

"You have my heartfelt agreement there, ma'am!"

THE COUNCIL CHAMBER, WHITEHALL PALACE, 3PM, 6 DECEMBER 1546

Archbishop Cranmer opens the meeting.

"Thank you, my Lords and Gentlemen, for attending at very short notice. There are seven of us here which is legally enough for a quorum. I've been asked to chair the meeting, as I was summoned over here across the river early this morning. As I'm sure you all know, the King's Grace was struck down by a seizure yesterday evening. It was so bad that he couldn't move his right arm, and – much worse – completely lost the power of speech. Doctors, of course, have been working hard to restore these basic abilities. And my latest news is that his right arm has already recovered, and his speech has been improving all day. The chief doctor says that the speed of recovery from a seizure is the most important augury of a full return to health. So it seems that the immediate danger is over. For which we heartily thank God. I would now like to hear your reactions to this unprecedented situation. Yes, Dudley?"

"It is a terrible shock for us and for our country. Speaking as Lord High Admiral I feel very apprehensive, and the word that springs to mind is 'rudderless'. For the time being, anyway, we have lost our strong helmsman. And his successor is far too young to take over. This is an emergency. My own response is that a new body needs to be set up as soon as possible ready to hold the reins of government. I will now make way for Paget."

"Thank you. I completely endorse Dudley's view. Obviously the best outcome would be the King's health, which we all pray for. But his return to health may not be immediate. We have no structure in place to deal with this crisis. We must set one up."

"Thank you, Paget. I now call on Lord Chancellor Wriothesley to speak."

"I agree, Sirs, that special measures are needed for this unexpected blow. But, surely, this Council of ours could carry on the business of State. The King himself chose us as a group well-balanced between reformists and those of more traditional beliefs. So we would be honouring His Majesty's own choice. I see that Bishop Gardiner supports my views."

"But, Lord Chancellor," says the Earl of Hertford, "This Council is only an advisory Council. The King is our usual Chairman, and we members can only advise him, not wield real power. Any new structure would have to have independent control. That control would be on stand-by. But it would leap into life at once on behalf of either a sick King or a Prince of Wales under the age of eighteen. It could be known as 'The Council of Regency'. It would not necessarily have the same membership as this Privy Council. Obviously, we all hope and pray that it will not be needed. If the King recovers, he would need to consent to its establishment. It would surely give His Majesty peace of mind about the future, after this appalling shock."

"You have clearly given much thought to our predicament, Hertford", says Cranmer, "To me your description certainly sounds fit for purpose. We haven't yet heard from you, Sir Anthony – do you have any comments on the proposed Council of Regency?"

"Thank you, Archbishop. Less than twenty-four hours ago our King was laid low by a dangerous illness, and his successor is far too young to take over. So, I support the practical concept of a council of regency, as the Earl of Hertford has outlined. I should add that the doctors warn that, if anyone has had one seizure, they are more likely to suffer another one. In the past I can't imagine that His Majesty would ever have agreed to a council of regency. It's too early to say whether his seizure has changed his attitude."

There was an uneasy silence.

"It will take courage to broach the subject," said Hertford, "But the King will be more likely to accept a council of regency while he is still weak. So, I propose that the matter should be raised with him as soon as possible. Perhaps, Archbishop, you and Denny should confer urgently with the Queen about it?"

"I will do so, Hertford. None of us will envy whoever has to introduce the idea to the King. But I need to know whether you are all in favour of a council of regency? Thank you. I will be leading prayers for His Majesty in the chapel at 6 pm."

ENFIELD MANOR, THE COURTYARD, 4PM, 6 DECEMBER 1546

"Hello there, Joseph. What a dark afternoon! Come in and get warm. You know I sometimes see myself in summer as a post-rider. But not in December. Anything for us?"

"Just two, Master Ashley. But big news from London: the King's very ill. I've been riding extra quick to get here in daylight. It's lucky Enfield's not too far. Yes, the Archbishop's at his bedside, and doctors scurrying about. The Court's buzzing with it. Word has it that he's deaf, dumb, and blind."

"No! What a shock. Mind you, he hadn't been himself for a long time."

"No. They kept the lid on it. Kept telling us he was getting better. Do you remember Scotland four years ago, Master Ashley? Their King – a young man – died suddenly, leaving a six-day-old baby – a girl at that! I thought then, what a disaster for them. And King Henry often attacked Scotland then. They say that he wanted that baby to marry our Prince Edward. And now here we are in trouble ourselves."

"Just so. It's a bad fault line in our State. Actually, we once had a baby king, Henry VI. And a 10-year old, Richard II. Their uncles took over. But powerful Lords muscled in, and eventually both Kings were deposed and civil wars erupted. And then, you'll remember, there were the little Princes in the Tower and their really wicked uncle: another civil war! Not good. We haven't learnt from it."

"Well, I thought you ought to know. What with our Princess here, and you all stuck out in the countryside. I won't tell her, of course. But she's a sharp one; she'll soon pick up on any hint of trouble. Don't let on to anyone that I told the news, will you, sir? In my job I'm meant to be very discreet."

"No, I wouldn't. In fact, we're a very female Household here now, so I wouldn't want to alarm them. I'll just have to keep it to myself and wait for more news. But thanks for the warning."

"Do you think I should tell Master Ascham, when I go to Hertford tomorrow?"

"No. The uncles wouldn't like it. They like to be in control. Go down to the kitchen now and get some hot food."

LADY ELIZABETH'S QUARTERS, ENFIELD MANOR, SOON AFTERWARDS

"**O**h John! Look at you, spattered with mud. It's dirty weather to be wanting to ride. You shouldn't come in here like that."

"Sorry, Kat, I'm on my way to change. I just wanted to drop in the letters. Please excuse this intrusion, Your Highness."

"As it's you, Mr Ashley. Are the letters for me?"

"One for you, Ma'am, and one for Lady Tyrwhit here."

"Oh no. It's from the Queen. Come to my chamber, Kat, and we'll read it there alone."

"She wrote it yesterday morning. I'm sure it's my betrothal again. I've been dreading this so much." She shuts her eyes briefly. "But there it is. I can't stop it. I'm a prisoner really."

"Well, let's see what she says, shall we?"

Whitehall Palace, 5th December 1546

To Her Grace The Lady Elizabeth

'Dear Elizabeth

Following the very successful ambassadors' reception, given by The King's Grace, I can now tell you that His Majesty has received three offers for your hand in marriage. Those three are States which follow the Reformed Religion, so an alliance will be of mutual benefit. The States are Denmark, Strasbourg, and Brunswick. I hope, my dear, you will feel very gratified by this interest, which the King has generated.

After Christmas, negotiations about your dowry and other financial conditions will commence. Finally, His

Majesty will select the most suitable contender.

You may like to help me choose some English attendants to serve you at your new Court, including, of course, Mrs. Ashley. And after Christmas I will find a German or Danish tutor for you, which will certainly raise your confidence in your new life. We should also find out about their fashions of dress, before we prepare your new wardrobe.

I hope, my dear Elizabeth, to see you at Court before long.

Catherine, the Queen.'

"It seems horribly real and close with those names. I can't change my feelings, can I? I'm still so frightened and sad."

"I know, I know. I wish you were older, my dear. But the Queen is doing her best to smooth your path a bit."

"And why doesn't she invite us for Christmas? I've always been to London for Christmas. Or Hampton Court or Greenwich. She can't have forgotten about that. She's the one who arranges it all months ahead. It will be my last Christmas in England! What's going on?"

"Yes, I've been noticing that. But it's not for me to criticise the Queen."

"Well, now that I'm grown up, I want to know. I'll have to answer the letter tomorrow, so I'll add a question about Christmas."

THE QUEEN'S APARTMENTS, WHITEHALL PALACE, 7 DECEMBER 1546

The Queen is sitting by the fire, having listened to the Archbishop and Sir Anthony. She says wearily, "It's a great relief to me that The Council has devised this plan so promptly. But, as you say, His Majesty will have to approve it. We can't predict his reaction. But I do know that he would not accept it, if I were to try to persuade him. You will have noticed that the King very much resents advice from women. As you know, only this July he nearly sent me to The Tower. He had been persuaded that I was trying to instruct him about religion. Wriothesley and Bishop Gardiner were behind it. I only escaped that horror because I found out that the King had signed a warrant for my arrest. I was terrified. I went to him in tears. He accused me of preaching to him. I explained that I'd only discussed religion so that I could learn from him himself what to believe. Also that I had hoped that our conversations would help take his mind off his leg pains. He then said, 'Is that so, Kate? Then we are friends again.' The next day when Wriothesley and forty guards came to arrest me, the King angrily sent them packing and tore up the warrant. Since then I have never, ever, tried to persuade or convince him on any matter."

"Your Majesty", says Cranmer, "The Council would not wish that upon you. I too was nearly sent to The Tower, last year. Again by Wriothesley and Gardiner, who dislike my reforming principles. The King's Grace himself warned me of their intentions. He gave me his signet ring to show my enemies when they came to arrest me."

"Archbishop", says Sir Anthony, "the King trusts and protects you. I believe he trusts me too. But he would not readily take advice from me. He gives the orders, and my job is to carry them out. His eyes would certainly narrow if I deviated from that pattern. So, with great respect, Lord Archbishop, I suggest that you should be the man to induce His Majesty to set up a Council of Regency."

"Amen to that", says the Queen.

"Thank you for your faith in me", says Cranmer wryly. "Let's all hope I can do it justice. I shall pray this morning that God will find the words for me to carry it through. Then I will visit His Majesty this afternoon. I trust you will hover in the background, Sir Anthony."

THE KING'S PRIVY CHAMBER, LATER

Cranmer kneels by the King's bedside, and delivers a short prayer of thanks. Then he rises and bows low. "Your Majesty. I am very aware of God's mercy to us all in restoring your health."

"Yes, Thomas", murmurs the King. "Thank God. I've got my speech back." He pauses for breath. "But my right hand is so feeble. I feel exhausted."

"Your Majesty, you are recovering against all the odds. It is a miracle. But I can see that you are very tired. And the doctors have warned me you might suffer another seizure if you try to do too much too soon. We must conserve your strength. With that caution in mind, your Privy Council met yesterday. They deputed me to respectfully ask you to set up, in reserve, a council of regency. The purpose of this is to support our great treasure, the Prince of Wales. If, in your great magnanimity, you make this provision to support our Prince, you will be protecting not only him but also our country. The risk of civil war will be removed. Indeed, your own great reputation as a strong and wise monarch will be even more enhanced. Speaking as a Churchman, the sacred words of our Lord Jesus come to mind: '*Blessed are the Peacemakers, for they shall be called the Children of God.*' Your Majesty, I would humbly urge you to accept your Privy Council's request. A council of regency will take pressure off you, while you can rest, to regain your full health."

The King closes his small eyes for a few minutes, and just breathes huskily. Then he says with a sagging voice, "I could argue with you, Thomas. But I couldn't argue with another seizure." Another long pause. "Draw up a document for me to sign, Denny."

THE EARL OF HERTFORD'S HOUSE, 9 DECEMBER 1546

"What's the latest news then, Tom?"

"Good news, My Lord Ned. The King has sent Norfolk to the Tower."

"My God! Surrey yes, Norfolk no. That's what I thought."

"Word is that the King was asking his doctors what had caused his seizure. They said it was his mighty responsibilities and a very rich diet. The King seized on that as a hint of poisoning. He said it was probably Norfolk's revenge for Surrey being arrested. He's flailing about like a wounded bear at the bear-baiting."

"Very dangerous mood. We must keep a low profile. Not arouse any jealousy. Keep your mouth shut at Court, Tom. No gloating over Norfolk."

"Same to you, Ned. You treat me like a schoolboy."

"Alright, alright. We must both be extra cautious. We should stop going to see Edward for the moment too. It might be interpreted as feathering our nest for the future. Raising our eyes too far ahead."

"I'll think about that one."

"We've got to keep together on all this, Tom. We've come a long way. But the King's so dangerous now. He sees plots everywhere. We could be the next ones suspected of poisoning him."

"He wouldn't bother with me. I'm a nobody – not even on the Privy Council."

"So you often say, Tom. But I wouldn't count on that now. Just don't attract attention, eh?"

LADY ELIZABETH'S QUARTERS, ENFIELD MANOR, 14 DECEMBER 1546

"Another letter from the Queen, my dear."

"Ah! I've had a long wait for this. But the King's illness must have delayed it. Let's see."

Whitehall Palace, 13th December 1546.

To Her Grace The Lady Elizabeth

Her Majesty the Queen has asked me to respond to your letter of 7th December.

She has been deeply concerned by the King's serious illness, and Christmas festivities are naturally far from her thoughts. She reminds you that it is her prerogative to decide on the venue and guests for such festivities.

Regarding your betrothal, Her Majesty informs you that the King is still eager to retain control of the dowry negotiations which will soon begin.

With kind remembrances,
Lady Anne Herbert
(on behalf of the Queen)

"So, Kat, I am rebuked for my questions about Christmas. I was unlucky in my timing. But I hadn't learnt then that the King was so ill. If I can't go to London, I'd like to be with Edward, but I can't ask any favours now, can I?"

"Better not, I think. Perhaps a note of apology, explaining that we get news late out here?"

"Yes. I'll do that. As for the dreaded betrothal, that just gallops on regardless. What does Christmas matter to me?"

Kat puts an arm around Elizabeth's small shoulders. "You know, I'm beginning to think it's this waiting time that's the worst of it. Probably in a few years you'll be proud of your new country. And have a family of your own to love there. "

"There's no way out. I'm always sad now."

THE QUEEN'S ANTECHAMBER,
18 DECEMBER 1546

Sir Anthony Denny bows before the Queen. She is sitting straight-backed, elegant as usual, near the fire with two Ladies-in-waiting. Her chaplain is just leaving after morning prayers.

"Well, Sir Anthony, we are entering the last week of Advent. It will comfort us all to remember the birth of Our Lord Jesus

Christ, God's great gift to the world. I've been considering your question about how the Court should observe Christmas this year. I'm in no doubt that our celebration must be very restrained. The sad fact is that the King is fifty-five and he is not yet regaining his health. In spite of all the doctors' 'cures', his legs are more ulcerated than ever. And the seizure has exhausted him. So I've decided that there will be no masques, dancing or banquets. Prayers for His Majesty will be conducted daily. The Prince of Wales will remain at Hertford Castle. Lady Elizabeth will remain at Enfield. She will be happier there than in this sombre atmosphere. I had a kind letter from her the other day. Lady Mary will represent the King's family here, and keep me company at Court. She supports me about Christmas."

"Thank you, Your Majesty, for settling all these matters. I will tell the Master of the Revels. One last question (outside my remit) concerns the negotiations for the betrothal of The Lady Elizabeth. The ambassadors are concerned, and have been asking about the timetable."

"I've been worrying about that. It is, of course, a matter of State, but also a family matter. It has been a very personal project for the King. So it should not be delegated to the Council. I know that the King intended to be in charge of the financial negotiations himself. He said that the three States who are bidding for Elizabeth's hand are much less powerful than England. So Elizabeth would be a great prize for the winner: a guarantee of a strong defensive alliance with us. His Majesty explained to me that any dowry he provided for her should therefore be a small one. He reminded me that he himself had waived the need for any dowry at all when he was seeking to marry Princess Cristina of Denmark back in 1539. I gathered that his choice of a husband for Elizabeth would hinge on what claims for dowry the three contenders would make. The King, of course, is an excellent negotiator."

"None better, ma'am."

"But, because at this moment the King has not the energy to negotiate, I think I can dare to authorise a short postponement in the proceedings. Perhaps a month? The purpose of that – bear witness, Sir Anthony – is that it will give the King a pause to recover his health, so that he himself can take up the reins again. He would not want anyone else to deputise for him. For that reason alone, Sir Anthony, the ambassadors will have to be patient. I authorise you to communicate the delay to them."

"Thank you ma'am. I will do that. But, as you said, this is a family matter. I can take no part in your decision."

"But you would at least confirm my reason for allowing a delay?"

"Yes. I think that might be possible, ma'am."

ENFIELD MANOR, 20 DECEMBER 1546

Elizabeth, Kat and Lady Tyrwhit are sitting round the fire with their needlework.

Elizabeth suddenly sighs and puts down her sewing. "It's so dark here now! Why can't we have more torches and candles on the walls? When we had Christmas at Court, there was far more light. It's hard to read or do my embroidery after four o'clock. And after that I can only worry about next year."

"I suppose," says Kat, "we've been spoilt by always having a dazzling Court Christmas. It used to get us through these darkest days, without us realising."

"So, just when I specially need cheering up, we can't have a proper Christmas."

"Well, madam," says Lady Tyrwhit, "Tomorrow is the shortest day. Then the sun will start to fight back."

"And don't forget, my dear, that a few presents will be coming your way."

"Have you been hoarding them, then?"

"Yes. I'm keeping them back for you."

"Good! But we'll be such a small party here – just us three on the top table, plus John and the new tutor. I need more company, more activities."

"It wouldn't be right, madam, now we know about the King's seizure."

"I know. But we surely could at least have joined Edward. The trouble is, when I have no distractions, I can't stop feeling sad about my future."

"One other thought, madam, to raise your spirits, is that when you do marry, you'll become first lady at your new Court. Now here you could never be first lady, could you?"

"Well, no. There's no precedent for it."

"Exactly!"

"We are a very small Household," says Kat. "We're stranded, like on an island. But we get on well together, don't we? So we can only make the best of this Christmas. We must count our blessings, and pray for the King."

EARL OF HERTFORD'S HOUSE, 31 DECEMBER 1546

"So, no Christmas at Wolf Hall this year then, Ned? What used to be my dear old family home......"

"I could hardly leave London at this critical time, could I?"

"I thought our opposition was safely in The Tower."

"They were our old opposition. But new challengers can spring up."

"Nothing we can't deal with."

"No dukes to face now. But we new men will be jostling for position. We'll all be conferring."

"The others can't deny our family claim on the Prince."

"No. But we're not royal uncles, are we? Dudley's the pushiest. I'll have to negotiate with him. I think, as Seymours, we have the edge."

"Of course we have the edge. Don't be so damned nervous all the time."

"Safer than being so damned loud and impatient."

"I just can't stand all this waiting. I hate hanging back, loitering about."

"Don't I know it! But now, surely the end is in sight, Tom? Did you see the King's Will, published yesterday?"

"I read the important bits".

"He hadn't signed it himself, you know. Paget had it stamped with the royal signature. The King must be fading fast. Hasn't been seen for 10 days."

"Mmm. He leaves the Queen well provided for, doesn't he? Lots of jewels, money and lands including Chelsea Manor. Very impressive. And his daughters; each to get three thousand pounds a year, plus ten thousand pounds on their marriage to 'any foreign potentate'.

"Yes. Take note, Tom, that he forbids Mary and Elizabeth to marry without the Council's consent."

"Very well. That's the King's command. Long live the King."

***

Whitehall Palace, 3 January 1547

To Her Grace, The Lady Elizabeth, at Enfield Manor

My dear Elizabeth,

This is to inform you that there will be a short delay in your betrothal negotiations. The King is extremely ill at present, and is unable to supervise those discussions. The ambassadors concerned have been warned of a postponement until the end of January.

We have had a very sombre Christmas here, with daily chapel services to pray for His Majesty's speedy recovery. I have no doubt that your own prayers at Enfield Chapel have been in the same vein.

Lady Tyrwhit will return to serve me in London next week, and her place as your chaperone will be taken by my cousin, Lady Lane.

Although you are not living at Court at the moment, you can learn a lot about the formalities and etiquette of Court life from my experienced ladies. It is likely that I will send one of them to attend you in your first few months in your new home. I will have to select some more permanent Ladies to form your retinue abroad. Let me know if you have any preferences. I know you are very fond of your cousin, Lady Knollys, but she has such a large young family now that I'm afraid she would not be suitable.

I do miss your presence here, but in this anxious atmosphere I believe Enfield is a calmer home for you to spend your last months in England.

Catherine, the Queen

***

Enfield Manor, 6 January 1547

To His Grace, the Prince of Wales at Hertford Castle

My dear brother,

Thank you very much for the beautiful prayer-book with its gold-leaf illuminations. I will treasure it for the rest of my life, and it will always remind me of you when I am living far from home. It will surely help to calm my fears in that foreign world.

I have been using it to pray for our dear father, the King, as he battles against his long sickness. I've just had a letter from the Queen saying that he is extremely ill. So his recovery will probably be several weeks away. I'm sure you too will have been praying for him at Hertford. Everyone assures me that he will get better soon. God willing, we can all see him at Easter in a joyful reunion.

Thankfully, I expect to still be in England at Easter, 27 March in this new year. The negotiations for my marriage have been postponed for a month because of His Majesty's illness. It is a relief for me but not an escape.

I do hope you had a happy Christmas in spite of these difficult times. Perhaps your uncles and cousins came to stay? We were a very small Household, but enjoyed roast goose and Christmas pudding.

I hope we can meet at Easter, if not before.

Your devoted and respectful sister,

Elizabeth

COUNCIL CHAMBER, WHITEHALL
PALACE, 14 JANUARY 1547

rchbishop Cranmer opens the meeting. "Our sole and melancholy agenda today concerns the executions of the Earl of Surrey and the Duke of Norfolk. As you know, both are in the Tower, awaiting their deaths. His Majesty ordered their arrest for High Treason over a month ago. He signed the warrants for both executions on the 13th of December. He would not have intended this long delay. When he recovers, he will surely resent this Council's failure to carry out the automatic death sentences. I am informed that all the legal requirements are now in place for the Earl of Surrey's execution. The Constable of the Tower proposes it should take place on Tower Hill on the 19th of January. The Duke of Norfolk was arrested rather later, and the legal documents are not yet drawn up. His execution will have to be postponed. The Constable proposes the 29th of January. Do any of you Councillors have comments on these procedures? Yes, Paget?"

"My Lord Archbishop. This seems to me a very straightforward matter. The King's Grace made the decisions, and he depends on us to act as he instructed."

The Earl of Hertford rises. "Yes, it seems to me that we have already waited too long. The charge of treason is a matter of State. No acceptable evidence has been provided to deny it. Because they are of the nobility, the two traitors will have the mercy of death by beheading. I support the dates offered."

"Chancellor Wriothesley?", says Cranmer.

"I can find nothing to add, My Lord."

"May I ask you then to raise a hand if you accept the Constable's proposals?

Thank you. A unanimous decision in this grievous matter.

Finally, may I remind you that all Councillors are expected to attend the execution of our former colleague, the Duke of Norfolk."

THE COUNCIL CHAMBER, WHITEHALL PALACE, 8AM 28 JANUARY 1547

John Dudley is shown in to the dark chamber, where Cranmer is sitting wearily alone.

"Yes, Dudley, I have quietly but urgently summoned all the Council members. As you no doubt guess, King Henry has left this earthly world. He is past all his suffering."

"May God receive his soul."

"He died at about two o'clock in the morning. His breathing was very harsh, but he gripped my hand to show that he understood my prayers for the dying. As you know, Hertford had instructed me not to publish this news until the new King reaches London. That's why I did not summon you all here very early, which would have excited too much attention. Denny is keeping the King's groomsmen and the embalmers within the royal apartments for a few days. But it's not easy to keep such a momentous event quiet."

"So, our Council of Regency springs into life. Thank God we've got it."

"Amen to that!" says Hertford, joining them with several others. "Are we a quorum yet?"

"Three more needed", says Dudley. "Ah, here's Wriothesley, Paget and two more."

"I will open this all-important meeting", says Cranmer, "with a prayer for his late Majesty, King Henry VIII. '*Blessed are those who have died in the Lord; let them rest from their labours, for their good deeds go with them. All-powerful and merciful God, we commend to you Henry, your servant. In your mercy and love, blot out any sins he has committed through human weakness. In this world he has died: let him live with you forever. Through Christ our Lord.*

Amen.'"

The Earl of Hertford rises. "Amen. My Lord Archbishop, His late Majesty chose in his Will to be buried at Windsor where Queen Jane lies. On behalf of this Regency Council I ask you now to organise that funeral with all ceremony in due course."

Cranmer bows his head in assent.

Hertford continues, "Our thoughts must now immediately turn to our new King: Edward VI, my nephew. This Council will rule England on his behalf until he becomes eighteen. On my nephew's behalf, I submit that the Council will clearly need a leader. I myself am prepared to fulfil that arduous role. Yes, Paget?"

"With respect, Hertford, as you know, I helped King Henry to draw up his very recent Will. He definitely specified that the members of this Council would all be of equal status." Murmurs of assent surface.

"That was certainly so, Paget. In simple theory it sounds fair. But it's just not practical, is it? A leader is always needed to make quick decisions. Whole councils take time to assemble and debate. Those inevitable delays are not always conducive to the very safety of our realm and King. In the last few days I have sounded out several other Councillors here, and I've found general agreement. As for myself, I am one of the very few men who know our new King well, because he has been growing up far from Court. The only other Councillor who knows him is our Archbishop, and he is already burdened with the great responsibility for our Church of England. So, as King Edward's senior uncle, I propose myself as Lord Protector of the Realm and Keeper of the King's Person. I submit this proposal here and now for your approval."

There is a short pause, and then an uneasy murmur and shuffling can be heard. But Dudley and Wriothesley in turn stand up and firmly voice their support. More heads start to nod their agreement, and by the time Cranmer calls for a vote, a majority for Hertford is clear.

"Thank you, Sirs. A victory for common sense and strong government.

I now turn at once to our collective responsibility for the new King. At this point no word should be published of King Henry's death. We first need a few days' grace for King Edward to reach London. I shall set out at first light tomorrow for Hertford Castle with guardsmen to escort him to London the next day. He should arrive here by the evening of the 30th, ready to be officially proclaimed King on the 31st. He will take up residence in the Tower of London, as is the custom, until his Coronation in February. I'll send a messenger now to warn the Prince's – I mean the King's – Master of the Household to prepare for the journey. I'll also tell Enfield Manor to have a change of horses ready for both journeys. I shan't mention King Henry's death at this point. Meanwhile, Dudley, you should discreetly alert the Constable of the Tower and the Chief Herald. My Lord Archbishop, do you have any comments on these arrangements? "

"Not really, I suppose, Hertford. In these circumstances. I think your prompt planning does fit our present need. We must certainly show a united front at this historic time of mourning our late King, and welcoming his successor. One further point: with all this going on we can't possibly attend the Duke of Norfolk's execution tomorrow. Nor can it take place while our young King is staying in the Tower. I suggest it should be adjourned *sine die* for the moment. Do you all agree? Thank you."

LADY ELIZABETH'S QUARTERS, ENFIELD MANOR, 11.30AM, 30 JANUARY 1547

John Ashley comes in with a bow to join Elizabeth, Kat and Lady Lane around the fire.

"Any more news, John? You do look cold."

"Bitter out there. Well, at least all the fresh horses are assembled and ready to go. So the steward has fulfilled his orders. He's used to it. Enfield's always been a staging-post en route to London. Plenty of stables around and big kitchens."

"That's right", says Elizabeth, "Until I was sent here in November, I'd never lived here. It was just a stopover on the way to Hatfield and the other Manors. The others have much bigger deer-parks. I sometimes feel I've been forgotten at this halfway house."

"Well", says Kat, "we haven't been told to move on, so I don't know what all this flurry is about."

John and Lady Lane exchange a glance.

Not long afterwards they hear shouts and a clatter of hooves in the Courtyard below, and they go to the window.

"It's Edward!" cries Elizabeth "How wonderful. And his uncle. And, look, there's Master Ascham too. We must go down."

"I think, ma'am", says Lady Lane, "we should wait to be summoned. As it's the Prince of Wales. We must observe the formalities. I'm sure he'll want to see you very soon."

"Oh, I do hope so. It's so exciting. Actually I remember Edward was living here for several months last Summer. That was unusual, wasn't it?"

"As I understand it", says Lady Lane, "The King wanted the Prince to be near London. His Majesty was hoping to be able to make the journey to visit him here. But sadly, it never happened."

"Will they be staying a night or two?"

"I don't think so, ma'am", says John. "The steward had no such instructions. I reckon they'll be on their way again soon enough."

***

A bang at the door, and "Make way for the Prince of Wales!"

Three deep curtseys and a bow greet the cheerful boy and his three attendants.

"What a ride that was! I'm too muddy to give you a hug, Elizabeth. My uncle says we can't stay long, I'm afraid. But I'm so glad to see you all again. I've got to wolf down this bread and cheese quickly now before we set off again. That's what Uncle Ned said."

"But where are you going in such a hurry, Edward?"

"I'm going to London. I haven't been there for a long time. My uncle says it's a special ceremony for the Prince of Wales. It's a big surprise for me. I wonder if I'll get any presents?"

"Perhaps it means the King's getting better? That sounds hopeful for Easter, doesn't it? It's been so depressing with no proper Christmas. Why not ask the Queen if we could go to Hampton Court then?"

"Alright. I think I'm old enough to go there now."

"And Mr. Ascham's with you too?"

"Yes. We think I'll be staying in London a few weeks. Otherwise he wouldn't have needed to come too. But I hardly know anyone at Court, so I'm glad he'll be with me."

"Perhaps on your way back you could arrange to stay here a bit longer?"

"It would make up for today's rush. I can't really manage this sort of riding very often. Especially in winter."

"It's given you a good appetite, Your Highness", says Kat.

"Mmm – this is warming me up already. Uncle Ned said he'll be up to see us soon. Then we'll have to be off again."

***

The guards at the door announce the Earl of Hertford, who bows to the Prince.

"Well, young man, are you warm again and ready for a new horse? Good. Now it's time for me to make a very important and sad announcement to you. And you are the first to hear it. Prepare yourself for a great shock. Your father, His Majesty King Henry, died two days ago. May he rest in peace."

Elizabeth looks stunned, and clutches at Kat's arm.

"So, my beloved nephew, you are no longer the Prince of Wales. You are already our new King. King Edward VI. I kneel before you and kiss your hand. God save the King!"

Everyone else kneels down in silent homage.

Edward is dumbstruck, and gropes for words.

"But I'm too young. He was getting better. I can't – I don't know how to be King yet."

He tries to brush his tears away, and Elizabeth steals up and puts an arm round him.

"That's enough, Milady, thank you. You'll be glad to hear, Your Majesty, that I have been appointed Lord Protector of this country. And Keeper of the King's Person. That means that, with the help of The Council of Regency, I will rule on your behalf until you are eighteen. So there's nothing to be afraid of. Over the next nine years I will see that you are gradually trained in all the duties of a monarch.

Yes, of course, Your Majesty, you will grieve for the loss of your great father. But our immediate duty now is to ride on to London. Tomorrow you will be publicly proclaimed King by the College of Heralds. For the next few weeks before the Coronation you'll live in the royal apartments at The Tower, as all previous Kings have done. But we can't waste time out here. We must get down to the Courtyard. Here's Mr. Ascham with an extra cloak for you. We'll have better roads from now on." And his strong arm steers Edward out through the door.

The Enfield group slowly get to their feet again.

"The power behind the throne", says John.

"A bit more courtesy would have been welcome", says Kat. "No sympathy given to our Elizabeth's feelings."

Elizabeth looks dazed, and nervous rather than tearful. "I can't take it in. The King gone? It's so sudden. I never knew he was dying. What shall I do?"

"It's the shock, my dear. We're all shocked. Sit down by the fire, and Sally will bring a warm drink. That Lord Hertford has no consideration. He just rides roughshod over peoples' feelings."

"We'll have to get used to him, Mrs Ashley. I think he's here to stay. He won't appreciate criticism."

"Exactly", says John, "A new era begins. For the next nine years. And probably a lot longer."

"I don't want to know that, John. Those Seymours. You wouldn't think two brothers could be so different. You see, Lady Lane, we got to know them when we shared the Prince's Household for many years. The Earl on his visits always pointedly ignored Elizabeth and her Household. We were all beneath his notice. But Tom Seymour was friendly and cheerful, teasing us all, even Elizabeth, and making us laugh. Such a handsome man too. Alright, John, I've had my say. Now, my dear", she continues, taking Elizabeth's hand, "I'm sorry, I'm neglecting you. I got carried away. Let's go to your room, and say some quiet prayers for your father."

THE COLLEGE OF HERALDS IN LONDON,
11AM, 31 JANUARY 1547

News has spread in London, and crowds throng the street below, as the Garter King of Arms steps out on the balcony, heralded by a trumpet fanfare.

"Oyez, oyez, good citizens. Pray silence for a proclamation. Be it known that His Majesty King Henry VIII has died after a long and peaceful reign of thirty-seven years. I here proclaim that Edward, Prince of Wales, now becomes King Edward VI, of whose most lawful right and title to the Crown we need not doubt. The King is dead. Long live the King! King Edward is now lodging in the Tower of London, to await his Coronation on the 20th of February.

"Be it also proclaimed that the King's uncle, the Earl of Hertford, will take the new title, Duke of Somerset. He will be known as the Lord Protector and Keeper of the King's Person. He will lead the Council of Regency, which will govern during King Edward's minority.

"I also announce three further honours: Sir John Dudley becomes Earl of Warwick, Chancellor Wriothesley becomes Earl of Southampton, and Thomas Seymour becomes Lord Seymour of Sudeley. These Proclamations will be displayed on church doors in London, and copies will be sent to the High Sheriffs of all the Counties of England and Wales."

LADY ELIZABETH'S BEDCHAMBER, ENFIELD MANOR, 10AM, 31 JANUARY 1547

Sally is laying out Elizabeth's clothes for the day, and turns to see Elizabeth waking up.

"Good morning, Your Grace. I've never known you sleep in like this. Not since you were a baby! And the mornings are lighter now too. Mrs. Ashley's been in and out, fretting."

"Oh, Sally. I had such a bad night. I just couldn't get to sleep for hours. The news was a terrible shock. I just went on and on worrying. I can't get calm again."

"It's quite natural, milady. I was the same when my father died. How were we all going to manage? But God will provide. I've put some lovely warm clothes out for you."

Elizabeth turns her face to the wall for a few minutes. But then she sits up with great resolution, and summons Sally over to help her dress.

"I'll get your breakfast sent up now then. Do you want Mrs Ashley in?"

Elizabeth nods and goes to the window, looking down at the quiet Courtyard and the London Road in the distance.

"I had an awful night, Kat. Hardly any sleep."

"It's the shock, my dear. King Henry was such a strong King. And he reigned for so long – thirty-seven years! All my lifetime and nearly all John's. It takes us all some getting used to. To be honest, it's quite a worry. Going from a very dominant monarch to a nine-year-old. It's a changed world. What will our enemies be thinking? The King has kept us from foreign invasion all these years, you know.

He just had that one domestic threat, from the Old Religion: the Pilgrimage of Grace, from York. But, goodness, that was ten years ago. You were only just three then."

"I do remember going to London in a great hurry once."

"That'd be it. Even Lady Bryan was nervous and upset. She'd always been so –"

"Yes, Kat. That's all very well about long ago. But I'm worried about now. What this means to me. I've lost the main foundation of my life. I only saw him on special occasions. But the Court honoured me because I was his daughter. Will they still respect me now his authority is over? The old slanders may surface, suggesting I'm illegitimate. That I can't be in the succession. No, Kat, you can't shy away from this now. You've always said that I don't have any powerful family to stand up for me. This is that moment. Suddenly I feel quite alone. I don't feel safe. That's what the King did for me. He made me feel safe. I hadn't realised that before. But now he's gone, who will protect me? I know I'm grown-up, but I need help. I must write to the Queen, anyway. But is she still first lady? Does she have any power now?"

***

The Queen's Apartments, Whitehall Palace, 4 February 1547
To Her Grace, The Lady Elizabeth at Enfield Manor

My dear Elizabeth,

Thank you for your kind letter of condolences. I too send you my sympathy for the sad loss of your father. His health had been failing for many months. I tried to support him, to maintain hope, but he kept growing weaker. I did not want to worry the Prince of Wales or you with his relentless decline.

As to your betrothal, it will surely continue to be negotiated. Your father's plans for your future can hardly be swept aside. I seem to remember that our new King too was in favour of it. He approved the aim of England gaining a new Protestant alliance. Of course, it will have

to be delayed again, while a State Funeral is held, a
Coronation is organised, and our new ruler, The Council
of Regency, has time to settle in to government.

Meanwhile, I shall expect to see you here by mid-
February for the Coronation on 20th. I am sure we will
find mutual comfort in our grief.

I should say here that we royal ladies will not be dressed
in brilliant colours at the Coronation, as we will be in
mourning. Choose a suitable Court dress, and I will try to
find simple coronets from the Jewel House for Lady Mary
and yourself, to highlight your places in the new succession.

Catherine, the Queen.

"So that's the Queen's letter. It does explain why I didn't
know he was so ill."

"Yes. And the Coronation will cheer us up with all the
ceremonies and decorations. We need some diversion, my dear.
It will help us look forward again."

"M'm. For the short-term. But after that, I've still got the
betrothal looming. It won't go away. She's right that Edward
supported it. Mary doesn't want me here. Lord Hertford doesn't
like me. So I'm still as sad as I ever was. It's my dark cloud."

"Your Grace," says Lady Lane, "I know you naturally feel
very bereft at the death of his late Majesty. But it could just be
that the loss of that support and protection here might begin to
reconcile you to a foreign Court? Forgive my boldness, Ma'am,
but I'm trying to raise your spirits."

"It doesn't help me at all. I'll always dread exile, and I'll do
what little I can to escape it."

THE QUEEN'S AUDIENCE CHAMBER, WHITEHALL PALACE, 19 FEBRUARY 1547

The five royal ladies curtsey as they are shown in, and the smiling Queen glides forward to welcome them.

"Good morning, Ladies! How good to be together again. I've summoned you here to explain our arrangements for the Coronation tomorrow. None of us here has been to one before."

"Pardon, Your Majesty, but when my father died, most certainly I attended my brother's Coronation to be Duke of Cleves."

"Ah! Well, I'm sure we'll all be grateful for any helpful comments. Now, I'm glad to see that you've all followed my instructions about dress. Your gowns are suitably grand but also sombre at this delicate time of grief coupled with rejoicing. I suggest you also have extra cloaks at hand, because coaches and the Abbey are never warm. We shall meet downstairs in the assembly room at half-past ten. Two open coaches, decked in silver, will convey us the ten-minute, slow drive to the Abbey. I shall take The Ladies Mary and Elizabeth in the first one. Queen Anne of Cleves will follow with Margaret and Frances. If it's wet, the coaches will have their roof coverings. But there will be huge crowds wanting to see us. We should all acknowledge the cheers with smiles and waves."

"With respect, Your Majesty," says Lady Mary, "It's only three weeks since my beloved father died. I submit that we should not be enjoying the applause of the crowds from our silver coaches. We should keep a low profile. Just attend the ceremony without any public parading."

"Your feelings do you credit, Mary. I myself had very mixed feelings about this.

However, I have come to firmly believe that we need to put our deep grief aside for this one special day. We must be seen to be looking forward confidently to a glorious new reign. We need to give little King Edward our public backing. King Henry himself would certainly want us to support his young son on Saturday. So I do hope, Mary, that you can accept that our joyful welcome to the new King shows no disrespect to your dear father."

"Very well, Your Majesty. It's still against my principles. But, I agree, these are special circumstances, which my conscience could accept."

"Thank you, Mary. Also – remember this, ladies – we are all so well-known at Court, that we sometimes forget that the people don't often glimpse us. So it's important that we should all be on display at the very rare event of a coronation. Any royal family must always have great regard for its subjects. Thanks to the printing presses they are now much better informed than they used to be. Public opinion can travel fast, and is actually becoming quite a force. Finally, the Coronation ceremony itself has wisely been shortened, because the King is so young. We royal ladies will be sitting in a special box near the throne. So be prepared for quite a lot of scrutiny in the Abbey.

And that reminds me that I've found two simple, gold coronets for you two to wear. I think it's important to display your very high rank now, as first and second in the new Succession. Here – try them on. They won't fit over those French hoods. That's right. Tomorrow wear them with your hair done up behind. It will make you two stand out. And so you should."

THE QUEEN'S AUDIENCE CHAMBER,
WHITEHALL PALACE, 23 FEBRUARY 1547

Lady Herbert curtseys as the Queen comes in, and then embraces her. They are both wearing grand court gowns.

"Dear Kate! Everyone's talking of the coronation and how well it all went. King Edward has taken the throne. Long may he reign! The crowds loved your carriages too. I was at the Abbey doors when you arrived, and I could see you had all been thrilled with your reception. Lady Elizabeth was wide-eyed with excitement! I know her well, and it was lovely to see her so childlike."

"All the cheering buoyed me up, after months of fear and tensions. I hadn't expected such a surge of goodwill."

"My dear sister. You've been such a good, brave Queen in frightening times. And think of all you've done for us Parrs: there's William on the Regency Council, and me and Maud here."

The Queen puts an arm round her sister. "I'm very glad you're here now for this visitation by the new Somersets. I need you here as a silent support. Duchess Anne is a very pushy character, and I don't want to feel outnumbered. There are changes ahead. I don't know what to expect. I remember when King Henry went to France, and made me Regent in his absence. It was a great honour and – Ah- our rulers are coming. With a large guards' escort by the sound of it. We'd better stand to receive them. We should curtsey to him, but not to her."

The Duke and Duchess bend a knee to the Queen, who indicates their seats.

"Your Majesty. We pay our deep respects again to your state of mourning for the late King. However, in my position as Lord Protector I have to quickly initiate changes necessary for King Edward's reign. One of the first changes must be to reconfigure the royal apartments. It would not be appropriate for the King – still a schoolboy – to move into King Henry's palatial apartments. As I'm sure you would agree. He will probably be housed in a guest suite nearby, under our close attention. I myself, as Head of State, will obviously need to live in King Henry's quarters. That is probably until King Edward reaches seventeen or eighteen, when I shall transfer power to him. My wife and I have plans to build a fine new mansion on the Thames, close to the palace, which we shall eventually live in.

Turning to your own position, Your Majesty. I am informed that you will always keep the title of Queen. As you are now a widowed Queen, the correct title is Queen Dowager. The title of Queen Mother can't be yours, as you aren't Edward's real mother. Great respect will be shown to you, but you won't have your previous influence or responsibilities. Fortunately, the late King has left you very well provided for, with generous bequests of money, jewellery and lands. Your manors at Chelsea, near here, and Hanworth, near Hampton Court, will no doubt have great attractions for you in future. Especially now that spring is coming. You will no longer be tied to Court formalities. What a tempting thought! You are well-known, ma'am, as a great scholar and writer of Latin. So I'm sure you will bear in mind the wise old saying: '*Tempora mutantur. Et nos mutamur in illis.*' Master Ascham reminded me of that recently. 'Times are changing. And we too change in them.' I won't look too far ahead at this stage, but in due course changes may be desirable for all concerned."

"Thank you, my Lord Protector, for your concern for my well-being. I am confident that The Council of Regency will safeguard my new status.

There is one important matter which I must raise with you. It is King Henry's project for The Lady Elizabeth's betrothal. No doubt you have heard of it?"

"I do remember the King announcing it to the Privy

Council some four or five months back. Of course no-one then questioned it."

"The matter had progressed well, until the King fell seriously ill. The ambassadors concerned have been patient, but are now asking for a decision. The Privy Council was not consulted, but was kept informed. It was a family matter then, though with political implications."

"So I, as Regent, now inherit that question. It was King Henry's prerogative, and now it becomes mine. It's not really a family question any more, because Lady Elizabeth has very little family. Unlike Lady Mary, whom I have to treat with kid gloves. I'll give the matter my urgent attention. And now, ma'am, we must move on with our busy schedule. Easter will be held this year at Hampton Court, and we cordially invite you there."

The Queen and Lady Herbert curtsey to The Lord Protector, as he strides briskly out to rejoin his entourage.

"You were very composed, Kate. Well done."

"I've learnt to be composed when dealing with powerful men."

"I was simmering a bit. There was quite a lot hinted at but unsaid."

"Yes. Not spelt out just yet."

"I was watching the Duchess. He must have told her not to speak. She was looking around, on the quiet, in quite a proprietorial way. She doesn't like the tapestries."

"I wonder where I shall be lodged at Hampton Court now? Perhaps I'll have to share with Anne of Cleves."

ENFIELD MANOR, 27 FEBRUARY 1547

Elizabeth, Kat Ashley and Lady Tyrwhit are sewing round the fire.

"I keep dreaming about the Coronation", says Kat. "I suppose it was all such an exciting contrast to our secluded life out here. We'll never forget being in that happy crowd and watching the grand processions".

"I loved it", says Elizabeth, "It was such a spectacle. It's probably the only coronation I'll ever see."

"It must have thrilled our new King, Your Grace, to see how much his subjects honour him."

"Actually, I thought he looked a bit subdued and overwhelmed", says Elizabeth.

"Well, he hasn't been used to London and large crowds, my dear."

"Nor have I! But I like to make myself known to the crowds, and thank them. I want to make my mark. Who else will do it for me? And the Queen said we must try to please the people. Perhaps now I won't be quite forgotten when I'm sent abroad. In fact, just as I'm starting to step out onto the public stage, I have to turn away and leave my homeland. I can't bear that. It's nearly a year since I was told, but I still dread it. It's been blighting my life."

Kat puts an arm around her. "It's not really like you, my dear, to get tearful. You're a brave, confident character."

"That was before I knew I was going to be uprooted. Ever since then I've felt helpless – like a puppet. Or some innocent person walking to the scaffold."

"But, my dear, look how brave you were at Court when you met the King. You had royal courage then. You can rise to the occasion. We can't change your foreign marriage. But you can rise to that challenge. You'll be free there to build your new world. If you can smile and look happy, you'll win a lot of friends."

"I know I'll have to put a brave face on it. But I'll be terribly homesick."

"I wonder, Your Grace," says Lady Tyrwhit, "If Queen Jane's motto could guide you? It was, '*Bound to obey and serve*'. She had that submissive attitude – in spite of being a Seymour!"

"The trouble is I'm not that sort of a person. I think she was a commoner, but I've always been royal."

"Indeed, Your Grace."

"But I'm still a puppet. A royal puppet. Waiting here for the summons to London. And beyond."

THE DUKE OF SOMERSET'S HOUSE, LONDON, 2 MARCH 1547

"For heaven's sake, Anne, don't be so impatient. The Queen is much respected. It would look very heartless if I ordered her out of her apartments now. It's early days, and I need to get everyone on my side. It's a minor matter, and I'm sure it will resolve itself. She'll soon realise that she has no role at Court. She's lost her patronage as a doorkeeper to the King."

"She never had much influence over him anyway. I'm sure she'll dig her heels in. She's too arrogant. Maybe your dear brother could lure her away."

"He'll certainly be thinking of her again. She's even wealthier now. He's still sulking that he's not on the Council. Actually, King Henry wouldn't have him on the list. I'd have appointed him last week with the 10 new members if he would have supported me, as they will. But he'd just be always sniping at me, and causing dissension in the ranks."

"Same old story. You're much too patient with Tom. He's another arrogant one, who'll have to toe the line. "

"I've had to learn to live with him. It's not really money he's after. It's power he craves. Even if he did get a seat on the Council, it wouldn't satisfy him. He'll always be snapping at my heels. It's hardly my fault that he's the younger brother!"

"He'll surely have to inspect his lavish new lands in Gloucester. And he's Lord High Admiral now too. So he's got plenty to do. In fact, we still need a replacement for the 'Mary Rose'. How about the 'Anne Somerset '?

"Is that a joke?"

"Sort of. But perhaps in due course? Anyway, turning back to the Queen. The Queen Dowager. What about Elizabeth's betrothal?"

"I've got to think about that. Most of my decisions are short-term ones. But for this one I've got to look into the future. This isn't a matter for the Council. It's mine alone. She's closer to the throne now. Better for us if she doesn't marry till after Edward. I want him to marry when he's sixteen. That Scottish girl is still a possibility. But they'll need time to get a few sons. We'd be a lot more secure then. Mary would be in her forties – past childbearing. Elizabeth would be in her mid-twenties. I could review her case again then. Whether she marries abroad or not, I do not want her having sons before our Edward. She's got no family to protest. I'm thinking aloud here, but that's it in a nutshell."

"What about the ambassadors?"

"Not much at stake there. Those little Germanic States are not much use to England. No, we need to keep Elizabeth under our eye. She knows she can't marry without the Council's permission. And I control the Council."

"Last but not least, what about our own mansion? The gatehouse will need to be very impressive. I want a three-storey one, like Hampton Court."

ENFIELD MANOR, AFTERNOON, 15 MARCH 1547

John Ashley knocks and brings in the post. He silently shows Kat the Queen's seal. Kat shuts her eyes hard and presses her lips together.

"Stay and tell me about your ride yesterday, John," calls Elizabeth.

"Thanks, milady. It was very good. But I've promised to see the steward now about that wall. So please excuse me." He backs out.

Kat pauses a moment, and then turns to face Elizabeth and Lady Tyrwhit. She walks slowly across to their window-seat, and holds out the letter. "My dear", she says.

Elizabeth springs up and takes the letter. Her fingers trace the wax seal. She's breathing fast. "The summons has come. So it's all starting up again. I've had three months' respite. I knew it wouldn't last, didn't I? We'll have to start packing again."

"Let's see what her timetable is, then. She's more patient than King Henry was. She'll surely give us some leeway."

"I daren't even open it. I don't want to know. I feel a bit sick. You read it to me, Kat."

"Right. Here we go, then. It's dated three days ago,

Whitehall Palace 12 March 1547

To Her Grace The Lady Elizabeth

My dear Elizabeth,
*   I have been deputed by The Lord Protector to tell you that he has decided to –*

"What? - Listen to this!"

He has decided to cancel the plans for your betrothal to a foreign prince.

Elizabeth seizes the letter.

"What? What? Yes! I can't believe it. It's a miracle. All my prayers." She sinks to her knees. "What a mercy. Thank you, thank you, Lord Jesus. I thought you'd forgotten me. Forgive me."

She rises, and Kat enfolds her, patting her back, and smoothing her hair. They stand in a long hug.

Lady Tyrwhit retrieves the Queen's letter, and in a few minutes passes it to Elizabeth.

"Let's see what this is all about", says Elizabeth. "The Queen goes on,

Unlike your father, The Lord Protector sees no political advantage in such a match, and he has informed the Ambassadors so.

Good. So it's all official! Then the Queen says,

I believe you will be relieved to read this letter, as I know you were naturally apprehensive about a life abroad at such a young age. I admired the way you wisely concealed your fears from King Henry at the time.

No doubt a suitable husband will be found for you before long from within this Kingdom. Approved, of course, by the Council of Regency.

I spent a lot of time on your betrothal plans, trying to carry out His Majesty's wishes. But, though it has withered on the vine, it did enable me to get to know you. It brought you to Court from the rural manors, and I enjoyed your company. Another gain from the project is the dazzling portrait itself, which deserves to adorn royal walls for many years to come.

*The Lord Protector has also been considering where
you should live, now that you are grown up. You are still
too young to head your own Household. But, now that
King Edward has become king, it is time to close down the
rural royal nurseries for some years. So, the Lord Protector
has decided that I should become your Guardian, until
you marry or head your own Household. So, before long,
you will reside with me in my own country manors. Mr
and Mrs Ashley may attend you there.*

"That sounds wonderful. It would make me feel safe,
somehow, living with the Queen. She can help me as I grow
up more. I still need you, Kat, of course. But she knows Court
life. I need someone of high status to support me. If I'm under
the Queen's wing, I'd gain more respect. She'll be my anchor in
that new world. It's all been decided over my head. But, by the
Grace of God, it's just what I'd have wanted. There's one more
paragraph here:

*I am less comfortable here in the palace than I used to be.
There have been some insulting claims that some of my
personal jewellery belongs to the State. I very nearly lost
my temper with all that unpleasantness. So I am looking
forward to moving to Chelsea soon. I will let you know
when to join me, and I look forward to your company.
Catherine, The Queen.*

"So, we'd be living in Chelsea. Well, that's alright. It's very
near the Palace. I can still attend all the grand events there.
But, Lady Tyrwhit, do you know what she can mean by the
'unpleasantness'? She's not a quarrelsome person."

"I wouldn't like to make a guess, Your Grace."

"Perhaps the Queen will open up to me when I'm living with
her. I'm sure I'd be on her side."

Elizabeth suddenly flings her arms wide open. "What a wonderful day! The happiest day of my life. We'll have a thanksgiving service in the chapel tomorrow. I must write to Cathy & Harry and tell them I won't be leaving them. They're my best friends. You don't know them, Lady Tyrwhit, but they're my cousins. They're a bit older than me, but they've known me since I was born. Longer than Kat even. And, Kat, you tell Lady Bryan. I don't think there's anyone else, is there? After all my fears I'm going to a very safe harbour: '*He leadeth me beside the still waters*'. Doesn't that sound marvellous?"

AFTERWORD

The striking portrait still hangs in Windsor Castle. It was the inspiration for this version of its possible raison d'être.

There follows a brief look into the rest of King Edward's short reign:

Thomas Seymour married the Queen in May 1547. Elizabeth later came to live with them in Chelsea. But the following year, when the Queen was pregnant and sick, he kept going to Elizabeth's rooms, and trying to flirt with her. When the Queen found out, she sent Elizabeth away to live at Anthony Denny's home in Hertfordshire. The Queen died in childbirth, aged 36, on 6th September 1548 in Sudeley Castle.

Thomas Seymour then began planning a rebellion, attempting to raise men and money in the West Country. On 16th January 1549 he was arrested at night trying to break into King Edward's apartments at Hampton Court with a gun. He was charged with twenty-three acts of treason, and beheaded on Tower Hill on 20 March.

Three years later, after England had been beset by sporadic religious unrest and also grievances about the rights to common land, the Duke of Somerset was accused by the Council of Regency, of misgovernment. He was beheaded in January 1552.

John Dudley, Duke of Northumberland, became Lord Protector, but King Edward's health began to fail. In May 1553 Northumberland quickly arranged a marriage between his eldest son and Lady Jane Grey, daughter of Frances Brandon, and third in line to the throne. He then persuaded the dying King to make a decree which barred Mary and Elizabeth from the throne, and made seventeen-year-old Lady Jane his successor. Edward died on 6th July 1553. But Queen Jane reigned for only nine days before Mary's many supporters won her rightful place as Queen. Northumberland's coup had failed, and he was beheaded on 22nd August.

Twenty-year-old Elizabeth rode to Mary's coronation with Anne of Cleves in a silver coach. But the next reign was to be the most frightening time of her life.

This book is printed on paper from sustainable sources managed under the Forest Stewardship Council (FSC) scheme.

It has been printed in the UK to reduce transportation miles and their impact upon the environment.

For every new title that Matador publishes, we plant a tree to offset CO_2, partnering with the More Trees scheme.

For more about how Matador offsets its environmental impact, see www.troubador.co.uk/about/